The Ruby Ring
and the
Black Knight

Jennifer Hashmi

Cover design by Scott Gaunt - scottgaunt@hotmail.co.uk

ISBN: 9798655231764

PublishNation
www.publishnation.co.uk

Table of Contents

Chapter One

1st June 2017

Bridget woke with a jerk from some complicated dream about libraries. The front-door knocker struck again. She slid out of bed and ran down the dark-green carpeted stairs to the front door. The postman stood outside with a small parcel. She thanked him and took it into her parlour, as she liked to call her cosy front room overlooking a strip of garden and the village street. She had no idea who might have sent the parcel, or what it could be, so she put it on her coffee-table and left it to deal with later. Of course she was intrigued, but first things first, and you don't rush at little surprises. You savour them a while! She smiled to herself about the simplicity of her life, that the arrival of an unexpected parcel was an occasion for a sense of anticipation. Well it was! She was comfortable in her little cottage in the village of Tavistow. Her roots were here. Her father, Richard, had been manager of the estate of Ashcroft Manor close by, and she had grown up there. In some ways she continued to be the child she was then, taking pleasure in the small things of life, and happy in the moment.

Her father had a degree in ecology and she had inherited from him a love of wild life, and interest in conservation of the planet. On leaving school therefore she went to Reading University to do her BSc in environmental science, and later her MSc in environmental management. She had then been fortunate enough to be accepted as a research scientist at the Institute of Environmental Science in Cirencester, her nearest town. She rented a flat in Cirencester for a while until one day, when she was driving through Tavistow, she saw what was for her the perfect house for sale on Tavistow High Street. She drove immediately to the house agent to ask to see it, and was entranced by the view at the back out across the Gloucestershire countryside. After obtaining a mortgage on the house she had moved in in twenty-thirteen. It was at the same time as when her father was retiring from his job in Ashcroft. Sir Roger Featherstone, the owner of the Manor had died, and he felt it was time for him to move on. He had a deep interest in archaeology, particularly of the Roman era, so he and her mother had moved to Chedworth into a house neighbouring a Roman villa. He was ecstatic. He had taken a teaching job in a nearby high school, and her mother was actually taken on as an assistant in the Roman Villa museum.

Bridget had not visited the Ashcroft estate after that. It was now very highly developed, with a wonderful botanical garden managed by Lady Maria herself. In her care it had become well-known in the county, and of itself attracted many visitors. They could also wander round the gardens generally, and the horticultural section, eventually winding up in the Garden Centre to buy plants, and shop in the home store. There they could buy everything one could need for the home, and there was a children's section which sold books, toys and clothes. Eventually, exhausted, they could relax in the restaurant which served all-day breakfasts, and teas. Ashcroft was listed now as an important place of interest in guides for tourists. As long as her parents had been there Bridget used to visit and often stayed there for the weekend, but since they left there seemed to be nothing to go for. A nephew of Sir Roger's had inherited the Manor, so it had lost its' 'home' feel for her. The gardens were as beautiful as ever, and she herself had a hankering to work in a botanical garden. If she ran into Lady Maria, however, she had to stop for rather stilted small talk. Lady Maria was a very sweet reserved person, but she had never been able to penetrate beyond the exterior. She felt awkward in Lady Maria's presence because she could never fathom what on earth went on in that pretty head of hers.

After having her morning coffee, she used her nail scissors to cut the tape binding the parcel, and it was only then that she saw the parcel had come all the way from Cape Town! That was where her paternal grandparents used to live. Her grandfather John Kendall had died there in February, and her grandmother three years ago. It must be something to do with them. As she removed layers of tissue-paper she found that inside there was a polished rosewood box. Nice! She lifted it out carefully. The dark brown grain mixed with orange and red. How *lovely!* It was about four by six inches, and three inches deep. The lid opened with a single hasp. Inside, it was lined with black velvet and packed in a little more tissue paper there was an onyx and wood chess piece, a knight, and a lady's gold ruby ring. Bridget looked for a note somewhere but there wasn't one. There was a formal letter from a legal firm called Cliffe Dekker Hofmeyr, and the letter was signed Donald Cliffe.

It read,

> *"Dear Miss Kendall,*
> *You will have learnt of the death of your Grandfather, John Kendall, earlier this year. He left his estate to his son Richard, but this box was put aside and entrusted to me to forward to you after his death. He gave me no explanations, but you will probably know what it is about already. It comes with my good wishes. Your*

grandfather was a greatly esteemed colleague in our firm, and much missed.

Yours sincerely, Donald Cliffe.

Bridget was touched to be remembered in this way, but how odd! The ring fit the third finger of her right hand and she left it there a while, thinking of her grandfather. Had it belonged to her grandmother? No clue. And the chess piece? Positively weird! It had belonged to an expensive set anyway. She picked up her phone on a side table and dialled her parents' number in Chedworth. Her father answered.

"Dad? How are you?.........I've just received a parcel from Cape Town..........Yes..........It's been sent by a solicitor called Donald Cliffe. It contains a beautiful rosewood box from my Grandfather........yes he left it with the lawyer to send to me after his death. It contains an onyx chess piece and a gold ruby ring!.........Yes it *is* very nice but it's a bit odd isn't it? What's with the chess piece? Any ideas?"

They chatted for a few minutes, but Richard could shed no light on the chess piece. The box and ring were obviously treasured items he had sent especially to her. Or maybe the chess piece had just been popped in there so as not to get lost, and then forgotten? There was no way of knowing now. She replaced the phone, and put the things back in the box.

Bridget had never met her grandparents. John had gone to South Africa in nineteen sixty-six and had married a Dutch South African lady called Louise. They had never come back to visit, but there had been phone-calls from time to time, and she had talked with them. Her father, Richard, had left South Africa when he was eighteen to join Bristol University to do his MSc in Environmental Ecology. Students from Bristol had come to Cape Town on field-trips to study indigenous species, and their conservation. Richard had got friendly with one of them and the upshot was he had applied to go to Bristol himself. John Kendall had been solicitor to the Featherstones. When Richard arrived in Bristol they made contact with him, and frequently invited him to visit them. Eventually Sir Roger appointed him manager of Ashcroft estate. There he had been able to build on the conservation work already established by Sir Roger. John had been much involved in the affairs of the estate, as he had assisted in the purchase of a strip of land from the adjoining property. He had taken a great deal of interest in the work there, and became Sir Roger's friend as well as his solicitor. They had set up the Garden Centre and the Botanical Garden where rare species were cultivated in protected environments. The Garden Centre was supplied by plants grown in the horticultural section of the Estate. Ashcroft Manor also offered Richard opportunities to take part in environmental projects beyond the Estate in wildlife trusts and nature reserves. Sir Roger was deeply interested in all these activities himself, and applauded Richard's endeavours. They heard he had even told Maria he would have liked a son like him. As manager Richard had been given a house on the estate and the family had been able to settle there.

"Well, that was an exciting start to the day!" she thought.

Meanwhile she had to leave the house within the next thirty minutes to get to work on time. She enjoyed her work in the Environmental Science Institute in Cirencester. A lot of it meant analysing soil samples from different parts of the County to monitor changes resulting from global warming, and she worked at this, peering through her microscope as diligently as she could. It was not her dream career but she was gaining experience and earning a salary while she looked around. This morning however her mind was divided. She meant to keep the arrival of the box as private as possible. She needed to find out more about it, and that meant making enquiries. She sensed somehow that her grandfather had given her a commission. Unfortunately he had not managed to write anything before he died, but he had asked for the things to be sent specifically to her. She knew they meant something. The chess-piece was important. Whatever they meant the secret lay here in England. He had lived right here in Tavistow. She thought about her grandfather.

He was a solicitor. He had been working for the Featherstones. They were keen too for his son come to work at Ashcroft Manor. That probably meant the association with John had been close, and kindly. He had helped Roger develop the estate. They must have talked a lot. He had acted for them in the purchase of a piece of land, and had been instrumental in the starting up of the Garden Centre and nurseries. He had history there. She could work with that. He had been a young man after all, and his job as a solicitor with Brook and Taylor in Cirencester had been his first, and his only job in England. His father, Nathaniel, had worked there before him. The ring suggested a woman. It was a woman's ring. A love affair? She knew better than to speculate without any evidence whatsoever! Leave it for now.

She decided the sensible step would be to pay Brook and Taylor a visit. Someone there would surely remember his name. Maybe there would records of his work. By lunch-time she was in such a fever of excitement about the whole thing that she went to her manager to ask for a fortnight's leave. She explained that her grandfather had died, and there was work she needed to do on his behalf. He gave her the leave.

She set off immediately to Brook and Taylors. Their offices were just off the Market Place behind the King's Head, so she found a parking place further up the road. The offices were up some narrow steps on the first floor, and were glass-fronted. She could see a lady receptionist at a table between two doors. She went in and asked her if she might talk to one of the solicitors. Mr. Brook was out, but Oliver Taylor was still at his desk, so she put her head round his door to enquire. Then she signalled to Bridget to go in. Now she was scared! She hadn't prepared properly. What on earth was she going to say! Oliver Taylor turned out to be young at least, around thirty, formally dressed in dark grey suit and white shirt. She wanted to find out if they knew anything about John Kendall's work with them, and if they knew anything about his dealings with the Featherstones. How could she put it in a way which would not sound too outlandish? Mr. Taylor stood up and greeted her with a smile, and she thought he was probably used to all sorts of situations in his work. She smiled back and took the chair he offered. He was dark haired and slightly tanned. Holiday abroad? she wondered fleetingly.

"My grandfather used to work here," she told him. "John Kendall? Early nineteen-sixties?"

"Er, yes," said Mr. Taylor. "We have work of his in our files. He was much respected. Good to meet you. What can I do for you?"

She decided there was nothing to do but launch into the story.

"I wondered if you might know anything about him personally, or about work he did for Sir Roger Featherstone at Ashcroft Manor. I never met him sadly, but he knew about me and we talked on the phone. He moved to Cape Town after leaving here in nineteen sixty-six. Last February he passed away, and he has left me a rosewood box containing a chess-piece and a gold ruby ring! His lawyer, Donald Cliffe, has posted them to me. It is lovely to have them as mementoes, but I am a bit mystified. He left his estate to my father in Chedworth, but gave the box to his lawyer asking him specifically to send it to me after his death. There is no note with it, but I feel they must have had some personal significance somehow, and he had them sent here, not just to me, but also to where they belong. I may be romanticising all this, but he seems not to have been able to explain them? It's just a sense I get that there is a story behind this,, so I thought I would ask here first if anyone here might know anything about them."

She had grabbed Mr. Taylor's attention at least.

"You connect them with Ashcroft Manor I take it?"

"Yes they are old-fashioned, and the box, though not actually dusty has a slight musty smell, as if it has been hidden away. My father came to England when he was eighteen to do his MSc in Environmental Ecology in Bristol, and he was given the post of manager at Ashcroft Manor. As a result I grew up there. We had a house on the estate. I didn't get to know the Featherstones all that well. I was a child in any case, but

6

we went to dinner sometimes, and I have been inside the house quite often. They have a lot of this old semi-antique stuff. We haven't. The box and the ring hold memories. The chess-piece is a complete mystery."

"You don't appear to have them with you. May I see them? They might jog a memory."

"Yes of course. I just decided on the spur of the moment this morning to ask for leave so that I can sort of investigate. I will go home and bring them back this afternoon if that's alright?"

"Yes please do! I am fascinated! Thankyou for coming. I don't know if this might be of any real connection, but John Kendall and Sir Roger used to play chess together every Friday evening. Perhaps it was a keepsake?" Bridget gaped for a moment.

"No! Did they? Yes that could be really significant. There seems to have been a strong friendship between them. All the years we were there Dad was very close to them both. Mum and me not so much, but I was at school and Mum was working in town. Thanks. That's a bit of solid evidence." Mr. Taylor laughed.

"Well I hope it proves to be. We are now the solicitors for Sir Roger's successor, Sir Michael Featherstone, his nephew. Anyway, see you later."

As she left the Brook and Taylor's offices she knew what her next stop must be. She put a call through to Ashcroft Manor. A male voice answered the phone, and she introduced herself. She explained that Sir Roger's old friend, John Kendall, had died in Cape Town and she would be grateful if she might come to the Manor to meet Sir Michael.

"This is Michael," said the voice. "I never met John Kendall, but of course I would be very pleased to meet you again. When would you like to come?"

"Like, now?" she asked. "I live in Tavistow and am not far away."

"Alright, fine. See you soon then."

She had to call in home for the box, but was at the door of Ashcroft Manor in half an hour. The door opened, and a tall young middle-aged man appeared. He had dark brown hair streaked with silver. He was definitely distinguished-looking. He wore baggy corduroys and a brown sweater. He smiled at her in recognition.

"Bridget! Hello. I'm almost tempted to say you've grown! My memories of you are as a child. We haven't met in a long time. How are you doing?" he said. He invited her in, and showed her into a drawing-room. Nothing seemed to have changed much, she thought, looking round. The same fawn brocaded sofa and arm-chairs with gold trim, and modern cushions. The same Persian carpet.

"You know the house," Sir Michael commented. "We knew your father. Stirling work he did here. I believe he is in Chedworth now, next door to the Roman Villa," he smiled.

Bridget grinned.

"Yes he lives there half the time. He is teaching in a local school there. Mum works in the Roman Villa museum."

"What can I do for you? I assume you have come here in connection with his father, John." He showed her to an arm-chair by the fire. It was a comfortable room and she was glad they hadn't changed it much. Now she faced the next embarrassing interview!

"You and I used to meet from time to time in my Uncle's time. John made quite an impression here. See, that is his picture." She looked at the framed photograph on a side-table under a lamp and recognised John in his young days. Very handsome-looking too. A dish, no less.

"Goodness!" she exclaimed. "I hadn't realised they were so close."

"Oh yes, indeed," said Sir Michael. She glanced up at him but his expression was bland.

"He never returned from Cape Town, so I never met him," she said, "and they never came to visit. We used to talk on the phone of course. All the anti-apartheid uprisings were going on in those years, and he and my grandmother got involved. She was Afrikaans, but, maybe rather surprisingly, she was a passionate supporter of Nelson Mandela. My grandfather was a lawyer with Cliffe, Dekker and Hofmeyr, but he defended people who had been arrested under the Population Registration Act. Interesting times."

"Indeed," said Sir Michael.

"I have received this box from his lawyer in Cape Town. Apparently Grandfather entrusted it to him to send to me personally after his death." She placed it on the coffee-table between them, and opened the lid.

"I am curious about its' contents. There was no explanatory note."

Sir Michael leaned forward to look at them. He took out the chess-piece first, and examined it silently for a while.

"This is from the chess set Roger and John used for their Friday afternoon games. The set is upstairs in Maria's room. A piece is missing." He studied it quietly for a while longer, and then looked up straight at Bridget.

"It's a keep-sake isn't it? His, or his, or hers."

She looked at the photograph, and didn't say anything for a minute.

"And the ring?" she asked. Michael lifted that too out of the box and rolled it back and forth in the palm of a hand.

"I don't recognise it, but I think we can assume that this too was a keepsake. John seems to have kept them, probably privately, in this box, but wanted to ensure they came back to Ashcroft, or to you, or both. That's how it seems to me. The box hasn't been opened much. It has that old smell. I imagine the ring is intended for you. Would it have been my Aunt's, I wonder?"

"It might have been, but he doesn't say so. I think the chess-piece is to go back with the set," said Bridget.

"Yes," agreed Michael. "I know, or suspect more than I feel I should say. Roger himself could not bring himself to speak about it. There was love, and because it was deep and abiding we have not felt able to move John's photograph. Maybe now we will. Your visit here brings some sort of closure." After another long pause she said,

"I think I should not talk about whatever that was about to my father," she said. "These things were sent to me. Not to him. And I believe I should take the hint. I shall need to show him the box and things though. He might have some feed-back of his own, when he sees them. I rang him about them this morning, but at the time he seemed as baffled as I am."

"You are a very wise young woman," said Michael, "and I believe you are right. They represent a very private matter, and yet John could not just keep them in Cape Town for someone else to deal with. And he may have seen in you a kindred spirit."

She looked at her grandfather's photograph again.

"He was very handsome," she said.

"And with a gentle charisma, I am told," said Michael. She sighed.

"Yes."

"Would you like to come upstairs, and replace the chess piece yourself? I am sure he would have liked that."

So together they went up the central staircase, and he led her off to the right on the first floor. As she entered the room he indicated she found she was confronted by a large photograph on the opposite wall of Sir Roger and Lady Maria standing togther in the garden. They looked happy and relaxed in the sunshine. What caught Bridget's eye immediately, though, was the ring on the third finger of Maria's right hand. It was the one in her box. They had a small copy of the same photograph at home, but in her father's copy the ring could not be seen clearly. Quickly she diverted Sir Michael's attention away from the picture with a remark about the chess-set. Whatever he knew about them or thought he knew, she decided she did not want to draw Sir Michael's attention to the ring in the photograph. He opened the lid of the chess-box and it was indeed a beautiful onyx and polished wood set, with one knight missing. She placed the piece in her hand into the hole with a,

"There you go Sir Knight. Home at last." They stood for a moment enjoying the sight of the beautiful pieces, and remembering Roger and John.

"Well done Bridget," said Michael. "Thankyou for bringing him home."

"I should go now," she said as they went downstairs. She went into the drawing-room to collect her box, and shook hands goodbye with Michael.

"You live close by," he said. "I hope we shall see more of you."

After leaving the Manor she set off straight back to Cirencester to Brook and Taylors. She couldn't wait to get back to present Oliver Taylor with her news.

As she drove her head was buzzing. She was in no doubt now why John had sent her these things, though maybe she would never know the full story. John and Louise had rung them up from time to time and she had talked with both of them on the phone. She had in fact talked with her grandfather at some depth about his life in Cape Town. Maybe he had developed a feeling of trust in her, and she did not want to betray that trust. But Louise? Where might she fit into the equation? They had always sounded busy and happy, very full of the political events unfolding in South Africa. They had joked and laughed with her father. But they never mentioned Ashcroft, or ever asked after the Featherstones. She realised that now. She had forgotten even that John had worked with them. The sight of his portrait photo on a side-table in their drawing-room had shaken her. They had loved him as one of their own till the end. And what had Michael meant by "closure"? Some unresolved trauma, or passion? Yes, passion. OK, well if so, it must have been tangled. John had married Louise, had Richard, and remained in South Africa for the rest of his life. Case closed for him? No. Had there been a deep silence which he had not known how to break, even when sending her the box? Had he just left it to her to deal with, because he couldn't? Maria it had to have been, but how did Roger fit in?

Oliver Taylor was in his office expecting her. He had changed into civvies, jeans and loose green sweater. He was waiting almost eagerly for her news! She sat down and put the box on his desk. She opened the lid to show him the ring.

"I can't show you the chess-piece, unfortunately. It belonged to the set John and Roger used to use! It is up in Maria's bedroom now, so Sir Michael took me up to put the knight back with its' fellows. He did not recognise the ring. However.........in Maria's room there is a large photo on the wall of her and Roger, and this ring can be seen clearly on the third finger of her right hand! We have a small copy of the same photo, but in

10

ours you can't make out the details of the ring. So the ring was hers. The chess-set probably Roger's."

"And the box, his?" suggested Oliver. She digested that idea for a moment.

"Possibly," she said. "They've got a photograph of him on a table in their drawing-room! I never saw it when we visited. Maybe they put it away when we went. Not that we went very often as a family. "

"So what are you thinking?" asked Oliver. "That John and Maria had an affair? The problem with that is that it doesn't pan out with his photo being in their drawing-room! And Roger's own obvious attachment to him. And they took trouble to make contact with your father when he arrived in Bristol."

"I know. I can't figure it out. There are pieces missing. There's more to it, and I don't know if it has any importance for us now, or whether I should just let it be. I have returned the chess piece."

"Well Sir Michael seemed to be a bit concerned. He rang my partner, Francis, here after your visit to Ashcroft to ask about the rights of illegitimate sons to inherit a title or an estate! I shouldn't be telling you, but I am, obviously. Have you thought of that angle?"

Bridget gaped at him unable to speak.

"No! Surly not! Louise was my Dad's mother. He was born in Cape Town."

"We will certainly take that as the assumption, but why would Michael wonder so quickly if Maria might have been Richard's mother? That can be the only reason for the phone-call. In fact, if your Dad had wanted to challenge the inheritance, he would have had to put in his claim within six months of Roger's death, but that aside, almost immediately Michael is on the phone, presumably to check his position!"

"I have no idea. He gave no hint of that thought when I was there, but the implications might not have sunk in then. He did say there were things he knew which it was not his right to tell. Nobody would dream of wanting Ashcroft in my family. Nor would we dream of betraying Grandfather's secret, if he had one. It is certainly strange Michael jumped to that possibility after seeing the box and things. Even I had not seen that far, but it was entrenched in my mind that my grandmother was Louise. And I have no solid reason to doubt that."

"And you'll say nothing to your Dad?"

"Goodness no. It isn't my secret or my business, nor ever will be."

"Will you come out to dinner with me tonight?"

"Thankyou. I'd love to," she smiled.

Chapter Two

She returned home with a feeling of satisfaction for the day's work, and quite excited to be going out with Oliver. They were on the same wavelength so there wasn't the topic-of-conversation problem. They needn't talk at all really to be perfectly content. Of course what to wear was always an issue. A dress yes. She studied her collection and eliminated the non-suitable. The dark green wool with three-quarter sleeves? A friend had chosen it for her and it did look to be right for this evening. Non-committal as to venue, but charming as to look. Right, so now a shower and a long think.

Her head was buzzing with the notion that her grandfather had possibly had an affair with Maria. Might there be evidence somewhere of what actually happened? All the staff of those days would be gone by now. They would have known! Whatever she did would have to be very discreet. John had observed total silence on the matter for fifty years. He certainly had not intended her to betray them. He had protected Maria principally, and her father, and Roger.

Oliver drew up outside her house in his white Range Rover at seven. She slipped out quickly as it was a no-parking lane. He had opened the door from the inside so she slid into the seat and smiled at him. In her long grey jacket with flowery scarf she felt just about OK. She never felt sexy, or even fashionable. For her it was always a case of passing muster. She was actually beautiful with long shining dark blond hair combed up into a pony-tail and small gold ear-rings, but her inferiority complex about her dress-sense blocked any temptation to vanity. Oliver wore a definitely fashionable brown jacket.

"Where shall we go?" he asked.

"Somewhere in Cirencester," she said. "It is a fun town at night."

"Jesse's Bistro?" he suggested laughing.

"Oh yes! I love that place!" So off they went happily.

She couldn't remember when she had enjoyed herself so much. Oliver was funny and kind. There had to be a hitch somewhere. Whatever it was need not matter tonight. He told her his parents lived in Devon now after his father's retirement. He had a sister, Irene, who was a lecturer in English literature in Barnstaple. He had studied law at the University College London and then joined his father's firm in Cirencester.

"It was handed to me on a platter really, but I did grow up knowing the firm very well. I knew we served the Featherstone estate, but even now it is my senior partner who is actually their solicitor, Francis Brook."

"Was your father their solicitor in the sixties?"

"Yes, he was. But I never heard any "gossip", so to speak!"

"No, well nor did I! Do you know the estate yourself? Do you ever go there?"

"Yes, from time to time Francis has asked me to go and deal with something, and I have certainly explored round their magnificent gardens. I have met Lady Sandra briefly, but not enough to know her. There are two children."

"Yes. I didn't know them at all. That area feels like home though to me, so when I wanted to get a place of my own to live I gravitated to Tavistock, which is a lovely little village anyway. And my house looks out across fields behind. I like to stand out there first thing in the morning enjoying it."

"You must have friends around there too."

"Not so much. After school we all left to go to university or take up jobs. There's nothing in Tavistow, so we are scattered, though we keep in touch online."

"Where did you study?"

"Reading University. I had a great time but I wanted to come back here, and in any case there is the Institute here."

"You must interact with the government quite a bit. What their policies are currently on the environment will impact on what you do."

"Yes, it does. On occasion we have campaigned for the rights of the earth and vegetation." She smiled.

"Well it's always good to hear human voices speaking up for our land, but in the end the land wins. We treat it badly, it doesn't serve. Plants whither. Even the animals die. We don't call it Mother Earth for nothing," he smiled.

"Yes. At the Institute we study how to rectify social trends which have a negative impact on the soil."

"So you peer through a microscope a lot."

"I do. Did you want to be solicitor, or was it a case of training to take over the family job at Brook and Taylors?"

"Well the law is in my blood, with a father and grandfather in that line, but I like it. I get to study problems caused by poor documentation, or conflicting documentation, or even controversial documentation, where the laws have changed since a house or farm was built. You get to know a lot of local history in the buying and selling of property. Sometimes you have to plead a case in court. After that it is in the judge's hands, and he deliberates on precedence. He looks at what so and so ruled back in the year seventeen-eighty or something. It can be truly fascinating."

Bridget followed his account, bright-eyed.

"It's like that with us! We dig up history, not down to the archaeology, but nearer the surface where changes have been caused as a result of what people who lived there did."

"So I might even consult you when I get a knotty problem over who did what, and when!"

They laughed, feeling ridiculously pleased with themselves.

After the meal they wandered round Cirencester for a while and ended up in the Cerney House Gardens. The evening was a little chilly for the time of the year, but the sky was cloudless. Bridget could not remember when she had felt so happy.

Eventually he drove her home, and they parted, knowing they would repeat this again, and soon.

The next day she set off early for Chedworth. She needed to talk with her parents. They had been at Ashcroft from nineteen-eighty-eight, or her father had. They were married the next year, and she was born in 1990. She reached Chedworth in under an hour.

"Any luck with the box Father sent you?" asked Richard after coffee had been served in their sitting-room. She took it out and showed it to her parents. Her father didn't recognise it.

"No, I never laid eyes on that before, nor the ring," he said.

"I visited Brook and Taylors, Roger's solicitors, to find out any possible background. They are sort of semi-antique, and English. I didn't learn much except that Grandfather and Roger played chess every week."

"Right," said Richard. "So you think the chess piece was one of the set they used?"

"I know it was. I went to Ashcroft to ask. I met Sir Michael and he took me upstairs to show me the very set to which it belonged. I put it back."

Her Father exchanged glances with her Mother.

"My! You have been busy! All that since we spoke on the phone yesterday?"

"And you have come here to interrogate us?" asked her Mother, with a half smile.

"Now why would you use that word Mum?" she asked. "I have come here for the pleasure of seeing you of course, and to ask, delicately, what's with Roger and Maria, and my Grandad."

"And why do use the word 'delicately'?" asked her father. "I assume you have picked up on something we never in fact speak of."

14

"What?" she asked eagerly.

"Alright well you are a grown-up now, and Father was very attached to you. But it is private, Bridget. The Featherstones' business. Roger was homosexual and fell violently in love with Father."

Bridget nearly fell off her chair.

"No......really? Oh my God. So what happened?"

"I use the word 'violently' intentionally. When Roger discovered his feelings weren't reciprocated, as he had somehow fanaticised they were, he had a nervous collapse. Father of course left immediately. I suppose Cape Town was the farthest he could think of to go! They did retain friendliness at a distance, and they were kindness itself to me when I arrived in England. You know how happy we all were at Ashcroft. But there it was. Roger must have had to have counselling. I never gave any sign of knowing the history. One of the gardeners told me quite soon after my arrival!"

"But what about Lady Maria? They had no children. What a strange marriage. Nowadays there would be a divorce."

"Nothing about Lady Maria, Bridget," Said Richard firmly. "No-one else's business."

"OK. Well thanks for telling me."

"It's farcical," she told Oliver later on the phone. "Were they *both* in love with Grandfather! And they kept his photo on display in the drawing-room? That must have been for Roger's sake surely, hardly hers."

"What an extraordinary story," he said. "Can you picture the chess matches? Both of them gazing at John?"

"My parents said speculating about Maria is off limits. Their story. Their privacy."

"And no hint of Maria having had a child?"

"None. I have closed my case as far as they are concerned. We are imagining an affair because of the ring. I wished there was some way of seeing Dad's birth certificate, but there wasn't. I can never know if I am Maria's grand-daughter without seeing that. And I certainly can't apply for a copy. But he knows what's on it, doesn't he? If our elders decided to hide something I respect that."

"Good," said Oliver. "I agree. No good ever came from trying to unearth family secrets just for the sake of it. If you are her grand-daughter, he is her son, and he isn't saying anything. Louise was a good person. Committed to the anti-apartheid movement, and possibly risking her life for it, certainly her liberty. Both were supporters of Nelson Mandela and activists. You have more than enough to be proud of there."

15

"I do. And I am. I have always felt proud of them. Amazing lives, and if I have children I would much rather pass on her story of fighting apartheid, than a murky story of adultery at Ashcroft Manor! There is no comparison."

"Not murky Bridget! They obviously went through hell, but I agree the South African story will be more appealing to the children."

She laughed.

"What are you doing now? Shall we meet at Jesse's?"

Chapter Three

The next day she had a phone-call from Michael.

"Bridget? I wondered if you would be free to come to dinner this evening? My wife, Sandra, is dying to meet you! "

"Thankyou, yes, I would love to come."

"Splendid. Shall we say seven?"

Oh hell what shall I wear?

She put on a straight raspberry-red dress with short sleeves and a gold chain.

At precisely seven o'clock she appeared at Ashcroft Manor front door. It was opened promptly and she was shown into the drawing-room. Her grandfather's photograph was still there. A blond girl, Natasha, aged twelve, and a blond boy of fifteen, Jeremy, were introduced to her. Natasha looked reserved, Jeremy confident. Nice children. Sandra was tall slim, dark-haired and vivacious, and Bridget took a liking to her immediately.

"So glad you could come," she said. "I'm out during the day so I missed you last time. Would you like a drink?"

"Yes, if you have a soft one?"

"Of course. The children don't get alcohol, and I am a Reiki healer, so I don't want alcohol spoiling my vibes. Coke or lemonade?"

"Coke thanks. That's interesting, Reiki. I have read about it."

"Yes, the holistic approach."

"I like that," said Bridget sincerely.

"Yes. Of course they have to have had NHS treatment first if they had needed it. I don't start from scratch."

"No," agreed Bridget.

"And what do you do?"

"I'm an environmental scientist researching the effects of climate change on the earth and vegetation."

"Oh goodness. How wonderful! Would that be at the Institute in Cirencestor?"

"Yes, that's where I work."

"We are soul-mates then. Holistic includes the natural world and the universe."

"The universe too?"

"Oh yes. We are star-dust you know!" Bridget laughed.

"Of course." She looked round,

"I love this house," she said. "Posh, but very homely."

"Yes, it is, isn't it?" said Sandra eagerly. "I love it too. You will notice it is much the same as it was in Roger's time. And that's your Grandfather!" She smiled, indicating the photo. "Gorgeous wasn't he?"

"Yeah. I never met him. We talked on the phone. They were very much involved in the anti-apartheid movement, so didn't get much time for holidays I suppose."

"Yes! Wasn't that splendid of them!" There was a pause, and Bridget glanced at Sandra, only to meet her eyes looking back at her.

I'm starting to get paranoid, imagining people know something.

"Where do you do your Reiki treatments?" she asked firmly.

"I have rooms in Cirencester not far from the centre," said Sandra. "Do drop in there one day so that I can show them to you!"

"I will. I'd love to, and you can talk to me about star-dust. After a day poring over earth-dust that would make a welcome change!" Sandra laughed,

"I'm sure it would!"

The evening passed very pleasantly. The children, she learned, were both at the Grammar-School rather than in a private school. She told them a bit about her work, trying to make it sound interesting by giving them a little of the historical background of Gloucestershire, as it affected the land. They were intelligent and appreciated the link with her work. Sandra talked about her parents in Wales, and Michael about latest developments in Ashcroft. The time went by very quickly until she realised she should take her leave. Sandra begged her to come by any time, and asked where to find her in Tavistow. Bridget had not expected to enjoy the visit so well.

She rang Oliver when she got home to fill him in, and they agreed to meet at Jesse's the next day.

Early the following morning she was standing in her back garden with her mug of coffee in her hand, listening to the birds and watching the clouds, when she heard her mobile ringing in the kitchen. It was Sandra.

"Hello Bridget. Sorry to ring so early, but I wanted to catch you before you went to work ....oh you're on leave! That's great because I wanted to invite you to our Reiki Centre in Cirencester this afternoon. I am free from four-thirty. Can you make it? Splendid. See you then."

After a quiet day at home doing housework and some cooking, she arrived at the address Sandra had texted to her on Black Jack Street at four-thirty, and found somewhere to park. The Reiki Centre had a shop front with a door which opened into the reception. Sandra herself was seated at the reception desk.

"Hello! Great you could make it. Come round to the back. We have two treatment rooms and two therapists. Janet has a client right now. Come through to the kitchenette. We can brew coffee or tea there. She took her through to a small kitchen with a sink and counter, two stools, and a chair. Soon they were sipping delicious coffee from SpongeBob SquarePants mugs.

"So," said Bridget, "tell me more about what you do. How did you get into this?"

"Oh, my Mum is a psychic. She does readings. We are that sort of family. I'm not psychic, but I am sensitive. I pick up on things, but I can't tell you a thing about your life you don't tell me yourself. Mum can. She's quite dangerous! The police consult her sometimes."

"Really? I've seen a few of those programmes on TV about psychic-led investigations."

"Yes, it is perfectly serious and can produce stunning results. Or it can go horribly wrong. There is pollution on the astral level, so the psychic can pick up on something not relevant to the task in hand. She needs ultimate discernment to detect what is interference and what is applicable."

"Right. That's interesting. So it must be a bit nerve-wracking sometimes. If you get a thing wrong it could be disastrous!"

"Disastrous is the word. She always warns clients that they themselves need to use discernment, and not just swallow what she says as gospel! But she is accurate enough for people to keep coming."

"But you had enough sensitivity for you to put to good use," said Bridget.

"Yes, I discovered I had a power to heal. It is an energy which comes through my hands. Of course I went for training. Untrained powers don't deliver on cue. And in a place like this," she said looking round , "you definitely need to know how to deliver."

"So how does it work?" asked Bridget curiously.

"It treats the whole person, mind, body, and spirit. The aim is to achieve balance. My hands become attuned to the universal life energy, and I can manipulate it to restore natural energetic balance in the recipient. Balance gets disturbed by stress or illness. Sometimes people are just looking for deep relaxation. Sometimes they are in actual distress. I can see where the imbalance is taking place, and target the actual area of disruption. The energies flow back and forth between my hands and the knot until a free flow is achieved. Holistic healing looks at the entire person and what is going on in his or her life to cause imbalance."

Bridget stared at Sandra.

19

"Do you know, you sound exactly like Grandfather, John that is, on the subject of African mystical healing. That, according to him, is all about restoring balance. That was the very word he used to use."

"Goodness!" exclaimed Sandra. "Those must have been pretty in-depth phone-conversations you had!"

"Yes they were sometimes," she admitted. "I got interested."

"So now I realise why he sent you the chess-piece and the ring," said Sandra. "You were on the same wave-length, and he needed you to get it. Have you discovered what he wanted you to pick up on?" Sandra looked at Bridget shrewdly.

Bridget was quiet for a moment.

"If you know I don't need to tell you. If you don't I can't."

"That Maria was the love of his life," said Sandra.

Bridget was startled, but said nothing.

"It's alright Bridget. I do know. I keep it to myself. I don't know many details. If there are family secrets, Michael keeps them to himself. And he is entitled to. I never ask. Heavens, we have enough of them in my own family! You don't always tell your spouse everything. We enter marriage with all sorts of baggage, and it is too romantic to imagine your spouse needs to see it all! I never bought into that idea. Now, come and see where I work, and our Aladdin's cave upstairs!"

She took Bridget to the first door on the left as they left the kitchen. In the middle of the room was a couch with a soft green and blue cover on it. The window opposite had frosted glass and brown curtains. Round the walls small shelves had been placed to hold candles. On a table by the window an incense stick smoked gently. Beside it was a cut-glass bowl full of crystals. There were two pictures on the walls, one of the sea at sunset, and the other a woodland scene with the light shining down through the trees. The walls were painted very pale cream.

"This is lovely," said Bridget, "and the incense lifts you out of this world before you do anything else."

"I play gentle music if the client likes it."

"What a pleasant place to be!"

"Now I will show you upstairs," said Sandra.

They returned to the reception room and went up the stairs to the first floor. Here there was just one large room above the others below. Tables were set round the periphery and covered with black cloths. On one of them were arranged trays of crystals and gem-stones. On another candles of many colours and sizes. On another bottles and jars containing liquids or ointments, and incense sticks, and on another framed images of what looked like Japanese writing, along with framed wise words or spiritual thoughts.

"I love these things!" said Bridget. "Are they all for your use, or do you sell them as well?"

"Yes, we sell them too. There is a notice inviting clients to come up and see. Choose something. No let me give you something."

She pulled out a drawer from one of the tables and took out a cellophane bag and went from tray to tray of the crystals selecting about twenty assorted stones. Then she sealed the bag and gave it to Bridget.

"Here, take these and put them in your bedroom somewhere. They emit healing energy vibes!"

"Well, thankyou," she said, taking the bag. "They are beautiful."

She leaned on a table, knowing she had to take this a bit further.

"Sandra, how do you know about Maria?"

"How do *you* know first?"

"May we talk as confidentially as if I were your client? This wouldn't be something, for instance, to share even with Michael?"

"Heavens no. I don't tell him about other peoples' private affairs," promised Sandra.

"Well, from the ring really. It was Maria's. In a photograph in her bedroom it can be seen clearly on her finger. So she gave John her ring. He also had a chess-piece. Who gave him that? We don't know, but it is back now with the set as I am sure he meant it to be."

"And," she glanced at Sandra awkwardly, "after my first visit to Ashcroft Michael rang his solicitor to ask about the right of bastard children to inherit titles or property. I was told this confidentially, so please, not a word."

Sandra said carefully,

"So that put you on to the idea that Richard......?"

"Yes. Of course, just supposing, he *didn't* have any right after not claiming it at the time, when Roger died. I mean, I know he wouldn't have the slightest wish to inherit. That is not an issue. And for all practical purposes his mother was Louise. There was something odd about my parents though when I went to show them the box and the ring. They just told me not to speculate basically. The Featherstones' business. Not ours."

"So you are leaving it at that?" asked Sandra.

"Yes. I just have to be absolutely sure that there isn't some unfinished business in England that Grandfather wanted me to attend to. He gave the box to his lawyer-colleague in Cape Town asking for it to be sent to me after his death. No note. I do mull over it a bit. And then you speak quite openly about Maria being the love of his life! How many people know *that!*"

"No-one," said Sandra firmly.

21

"Except you? Ah. She came to you professionally," realised Bridget. "I can quite see she needed to. She had to nurse Roger out of *his* anguish. And with John's talk of 'balance' she must have been attracted to Reiki immediately. She needed a piece for herself. Poor Maria. Anyway, case closed, as far as you are concerned too. Thank you for sharing so much though. I really appreciate it. And this is a wonderful place."

"Sensitive as the situation was, maybe you need to keep alert for anything in the present which might need repairing in some way? Is there any pain or damage he might fear had been caused, which he had not been able to mitigate?"

"Yes, you have put your finger on my concern. Is there somebody somewhere who suffered, maybe unintentionally, as a result? Or is there something, even, I need to do?"

"Need to do......wait..... Maria died rather suddenly. She had a heart attack, and then a couple of days later a second which killed her. If your love goes to the other end of the world, you don't burn all your keepsakes do you? You treasure them. Just as John treasured the chess-piece and the ring till he died. Wouldn't there be amongst Maria's things some remembrances of John? Wait, letters! They wrote! Of course they did. Maria was unconscious in hospital. Did she still have his letters?" Bridget looked at her stunned.

"Oh God, you think maybe she left utterly confidential letters around somewhere?"

"She might have, and believe you me they will be private! I'll search the attics. They obviously wouldn't be in her desk. If they exist they will be in some very secret place. Will you trust me to look? No, you come and we'll look together. It has to be a school day. The children mustn't be around. I'll take a day off here and we'll look together. I'm living in her house, and do you know, that possibility never entered my head!"

"Yes. I'll come. What a good thing you thought of that! The idea hadn't crossed my mind either. Thankyou for showing me all this Sandra. I feel as if I've been in another world for a while. So refreshing!"

Chapter Four

By now it was six o'clock so she rang Oliver to ask what time they would meet at Jesse's. He said he was done and they could go straight there. By now they had their usual table by a window, and knew pretty much what they would order. Jesse's Bistro had a wonderful atmosphere, with a low roof and wooden beams, and flag-stone floor. Along the wall outside there was a well-tended flower-bed. Some of the windows were open, and fresh air combined with the smells from the kitchen, like in a comfortable home.

"Anything exciting today?" asked Bridget.

"No. Just the usual, conveyances, and wills. John's life in Cape Town has made me reflect on my own. Am I really going to go on like this, nine to five, for the rest of my life? And I think not. I want my life to have more purpose."

"What sort of purpose?" she asked.

"Something with real challenges that result in solid achievements." He looked at the bar counter. "I mean even those guys serving beer see more of real life than I do."

"Could you at this stage take up criminal law?"

"I would have to go back to the drawing-board, but I could. I'll let things simmer for now. How about you chez Sandra?"

"Oh, very interesting. Do you know much about Reiki? It is all about restoring the balance on physical, emotional, and spiritual levels. Grandfather talked to me about that sometimes in his phone-calls, but in his case it was about the restoring of balance of African mysticism. Of course the wheels in my brain started to roll. She showed me round. It's lovely. Upstairs there is a store where you and buy crystals and incense and that stuff. She gave me some for my bedroom."

"Did you get anything significant on John?"

"Oh yes. She asked me if I had found out anything more on the ring. She intuited a closer connection with my Grandfather than I had suggested. I told her how John had talked to me on the phone about African mysticism. Not your average phone-call topic, and she deduced correctly that we must have been on the same wave-length. She thinks he sent me the ring as some sort of token or signal for me to pick up on. That is how I have felt myself. Of course a note would have been great. I didn't respond much. So she came out with the news that Maria was the love of his life!'"

Oliver's eye-brows went up.

"Well that was very out-spoken. She isn't reserved like the Featherstones!"

"Not at all, though she is very discreet when it comes to her professional life. Anything said in her therapy room is as sacred as the confessional. I confirmed with her that anything which passed between her and me would be treated as equally confidential, and she said yes of course. She doesn't confide other peoples' secrets to Michael."

"But it does seem then that at Ashcroft they believe there was a love affair, causing Michael to call his solicitor to check on the laws surrounding inheritance."

"No. Think. Maria is alone with her pain, and along comes Sandra talking a bit like John does. She goes for Reiki therapy, or to unburden! Sandra is safe. She will never blab to Michael. It was my visit which worried him."

"So you think Sandra knows from Maria herself! How was it that she felt able to pass that on to you?"

"Because she realised I already knew, or thought I knew. Maria, John, and Louise have all died now. It has become history, though all the same she didn't repeat a word of anything Maria actually said. Only the basic information I might need to know, and which she thinks John now wants me to know."

They ate quietly for a while pondering what John might have intended Bridget to discover.

"There's more though," said Bridget. "Sandra feels there might be some unfinished business which John needs me to deal with. And then she had a lightening flash. She remembered how Maria died rather unexpectedly and quickly as the result of two heart-attacks. She was hospitalised and unconscious. Sandra believes, probably knows, there must be letters. Until I raked up the subject it hadn't occurred to her, but now she feels it is a matter of urgency that we look for them. She wants me to help her."

"What made Richard choose Bristol University? Who inspired that choice? So convenient for Ashcroft."

"Bristol sent ecology students on field trips to South Africa to study indigenous species. Dad got friendly with one of the students, and decided Bristol was the place for him, and ecology."

"His father must have been delighted." said Oliver, dryly. He looked serious.

"The letters could be shocking to you Bridget. I hope you won't get hurt."

Bridget was surprised.

24

"Hurt by what Oliver? An adulterous affair isn't such big news these days. They are going on all around and children end up with parents who aren't their biological parents. I am already prepped for the sort of letters they are likely to be. A question might be whether to treasure them or burn them."

"They lived their lives very intensely Bridget, on the edge. That is what I am realising now about my own life. It's too comfortable. How am I to grow, just sitting in my office at Brook and Taylors? Heavens, they had an affair under Roger's nose, flying in the face of the principles instilled in them in their up-bringing, and their own stern moral code! My understanding of John is that he was a deeply serious person. He saw his personal life in cosmic terms, for crying out loud! He believed in destiny and purpose. And we knew Maria, how delicate her conscience was, how afraid of hurting anyone, how she looked after those plants, caring for each single one, and we know she loved Roger. Yet there they were, in Roger's very presence half the time. Then to save Roger any more pain, and thereby causing Maria, his real love, ultimate pain, he goes off to South Africa! And he isn't just sitting there waiting for Maria to do something. He marries Louise! The next year! I mean what? And she made Richard a good mum. They all lived according to rules which have long been forgotten. Louise obviously knew about Maria. Seriously, I would love to understand more about that code. In Cape Town they forget their personal issues in their fight for the rights of others. They go against the flow again, big time, risking their liberty and possibly their lives, and in spite of having a child to protect. They never put 'me' first. It was always about what was best for the people around them."

Bridget listened to the outburst, almost shocked by his grasp of what it must have taken Maria and John to live their lives the way they did.

"And Maria turned to Sandra in later life, but when was she ever sorry for herself or unkind to Roger? She got on with things, and that Botanical Garden is what it is because of the work she put into it. Roger was a keen gardener but didn't have specialist knowledge. Maria somehow did. She knew a lot."

" So, you feel I need to keep this bigger picture in mind, and see things through their eyes if things look strange," said Bridget.

"I do. I think there will be surprises."

"And of course it isn't all about me. In fact none of it is about me. My job is to discover if there is anything which needs attending to."

"Yes. I wonder if I could put in a couple of years at Cliffe Dekker Hofmeyr's?" said Oliver.

"What?!"

"Yeah. The sharp edge isn't going to come to me is it? I have to go out and find it. Even Roger. Look at him! Gentle and mild and funny. And he declares himself to a fellow man back in nineteen-sixty-five. That's living Bridget."

Bridget was a bit troubled. This was a new Oliver. No longer the understanding confidante. The warrior in him somewhere had been aroused to look for a challenge and perform great deeds! Gosh.

She wanted him to be her ear. Listening to *her* things. That is to say, wait a minute, did she want him? Yes she did. But not tilting at windmills in Cape Town for goodness sake. She needed him right here.

"What's the matter Bridget?" he said, seeing the expression on her face..

"Oh, I don't know. You have every right to live your life as you want to."

"But you don't approve."

"Yes, of course I do. Who am I to approve or disapprove a decision of yours? It's just that.......well Cape Town is a long way away."

"And you mind that?" he asked, watching her.

"Well yes. What a long way away it must have seemed to Maria."

"Are we invoking Maria and John here?" he asked, looking at her keenly.

Now she was confused.

"You want me here," he said carefully. And when she couldn't reply he said,

"You want me."

She gave a sudden movement which knocked over a glass half-full of water. A waitress came to mop up while Bridget stared at the table-top.

"Just yes or no Bridget," he said as the waitress walked away.

"Well, I suppose yes. Yes."

"Good. Because I want you. How about coming to Cape Town with me?"

"I think I need a brandy."

"Seriously?"

"No.....give me a minute. Where are we now?"

"Living together in Cape Town preferably, or adding a chapter to the Maria-John story by writing letters. If you went you could even write an important paper on indigenous species." She laughed now.

"I have no intention of actually moving there. I just want to shake the bottle a bit. Cape Town should do it"

"Two years?"

"Well, alright, if you don't come, one year."

"And that would still be enough to shake the bottle?"

"Should be."

"But I'm not sleeping with you!"

"Good heavens no! Perish the thought!"

She grinned.

"I'm serious. I'm holistic enough to believe body mind and spirit should be in it together."

"And where might your spirit wander during sex? The mind can wander anywhere on any occasion as we well know."

"I guess one mightn't realise it had. It would be in the aftermath one would realise whether one had been in it in spirit or not."

"So, going back to Sandra," he said. "When is this exploration of Ashcroft to take place?"

"It isn't fixed yet. She will have to take a day off work because it must be on a school day."

"I can imagine. What shall we do now? Or rather where shall we go? My place or yours, as the saying goes?" As she looked a bit pensive he added,

"Not for sex of course."

"No. Let's go to your place then. I would like to see it," she suggested.

He led the way in his car to St. John's Road where he lived. Bridget was impressed. He parked outside a beautiful detached stone house with a metal gate. There were trees and a lawn in the front garden, and a bay window looking out over it. Oliver let her into a spacious hall with a Persian-style rug. There was a little table with a lamp on it and a bowl of flowers.

"Someone comes in once a week to clean," he said, "so I am saved that worry. Come through to the sitting-room. I'll make us coffees if that is alright."

"Yes, thankyou. You have a beautiful house."

He put the TV on, so they didn't need to talk. A re-run of "Dad's Army". Relaxing. He brought the coffees and asked her if she intended her work at the Environment Institute to be a life vocation, or whether she planned to move on.

"Oh move on definitely. I am establishing the foundations in the laboratory, but I want to get outside. So far, to work at the Westonbirt Arboretum would be my dream job."

"The Arboretum! You really take after Maria don't you, if you do."

"Yes. It does seem to be in my blood. If it is."

"And so, what about us? Are you coming to Cape Town with me, assuming I were accepted somewhere?"

"I think not Oliver. In spite of the chance to study indigenous species, it would break up my trajectory. I was serious really when I said I want to work at the Arboretum."

"I know you were. And you need sponsors and recommendations for field trips. It isn't that you can just go. And in any case it wouldn't fit into your plan. So we will write letters."

"I think that would be good. No skype or video calls. We sit down and think out our thoughts on to paper. Our serious thoughts."

"I do like you Bridget."

"And I like you Oliver."

Chapter Five

Early next morning, as she stood outside in her back garden with her mug of coffee, she had a warm feeling about the previous evening. How companionable they had been! She had never had any friend with whom she felt so close, as if they could say anything to each other. She sensed of course that he wanted more and so did she, but friendship came first. Never give your body till the man has given his heart was the wisdom handed down to her from her mother.

The next thing on the agenda seemed to be Ashcroft with Sandra. Her mobile rang in the kitchen, and Sandra it was.

"Hi Bridget? Can you come to Ashcroft at ten by any chance? Michael is going out and Janet can do my morning session at the Centre."

"Yes, I am living from day to day at the moment. I will be there at ten."

No need to worry about clothes for scrabbling around in probably dusty attics. Nothing very private would have been left in a bedroom drawer. Whatever there was would have to be in an attic. She had grown up with attics herself and knew the little hiding-places.

Sandra came to the door.

"Hello, thanks for coming. May we start with the search first and coffee after? You never know when interruptions might occur."

"Of course fine. The attics I assume?"

"You bet. Where else? We'll start in the back attics first I think. More sort of 'private'.

"The front attics are neat. Household surplus and furniture are stacked there. The back attics are where the children played. All sorts of personal and children's discarded stuff are lying around there."

They went up the two flights of stairs to the top of the house and Sandra led her into a room on the left.

"Loads of stuff in here. Jeremy and Natasha play in this room."

There was indeed. There were boxes and crates with cloths thrown over them. In a corner were children's things, an old dolls-house, a rocking-horse, a train-set, bricks, and dolls. On shelves books and jig-saw puzzles were piled. Bridget could see games she had also had, Cludo, a set of Ludo, and Snakes and Ladders, Lotto, Monopoly, Labyrinth, and others.

They stood looking around.

"Well obviously she wouldn't put letters in amongst this stuff. There has to be some sort of cavity somewhere. There are two back attics so let's take a general look round first."

They searched the first room very methodically, and then went through to the other back attic. In here there was a sewing-machine and a work-table, and trunks

"This is the more likely room for Maria to have hidden her letters. That sewing-machine was hers."

Bridget went over and put her hand on it and closed her eyes. Was this her grandmother's sewing-machine? Sandra watched her, understanding her thoughts.

"Shall we start on the trunks? Of course I have looked in a general way, and unfortunately the children have rootled around."

They began to lift the lids. They seemed to contain old evening-dresses, curtains, table-cloths and some crystal glass-ware.

"But Sandra don't you think that Maria would have put something utterly private where children wouldn't be able to rootle around? Like say the rafters? Even then a builder might come across them. I think the traditional under-a-floorboard place is the likeliest."

"And nailed down?"

"Screwed more likely."

"Alright let's roll back the rug."

They removed the trunks standing on an old red rug and then started to roll it back to one end. Underneath were bare floor-boards, which were not particularly dusty. They began examining them and knocking on them one by one.

"This was Maria's attic-room wasn't it? All this stuff dates back to her," said Bridget.

"Yes, I have it cleaned, but I don't want the things thrown away. Most of it is in good condition. It would be such a waste!"

"There's a loose floor-board here Sandra, and screwed down. You can see, it looks different from the others, a bit more used."

"They had no children, and I don't allow mine in here. I don't want them to start pulling things out of the trunks. Yes you're right. I'll get something from the sewing-machine to lever it up."

In one of the small drawers there was a small knife.

"Just the thing," she said.

"Maybe even the thing," said Bridget. "My mother puts all sorts of odd things in her machine drawers. There are picture-hooks in one. Let's see if it will do the trick."

Sandra handed her the knife.

"Your job," she said. Bridget glanced at her and applied the knife to the screw. It turned quite easily, and she pulled it out. Then she used the knife as a lever to lift the board. It lifted perfectly easily and, lo and behold, underneath it was a biscuit-box! No, two biscuit-boxes. Bridget lifted them out reverently and Sandra watched as she opened the lids. Inside there were several letters, preserved in their envelopes carefully and in order. In one box there were also two long official-looking envelopes, and a set of keys. Bridget's heart began to beat quickly.

"Sandra, would you look inside these please?"

Sandra opened the thin one first, and as Bridget almost half-expected it was a birth certificate. Sandra read out,

"Mother's name: Maria Featherstone. Father's name: John Kendall.

And the child's name, Bridget, is Richard, born eighteenth October, nineteen sixty-five."

"Oh my God. This is what we suspected, but to see it in black and white! So.......Grandfather took him as a baby to Cape Town. Then somehow or other married Louise, got Dad a fake birth-certificate, (Grandad, I didn't know you had it in you!), and passed him off as Louise's son. Heavens. No, he married Louise in nineteen-sixty-seven, the year after the new fake birth-date, December eighteenth, nineteen sixty-six. Why not put his birth year as nineteen-sixty-seven?"

"Couldn't Bridget. Think about his school admission. They might pass him off as a tall five year old if he's really six, but they can't pass off a seven year old as five."

"No right. Can you imagine the discussions! Louise was a brick wasn't she?"

"Yes. But what was in it for her, Bridget?"

"She was a really good person, Sandra."

"I'm sure she was, but she connived here with a respectable lawyer to fake an official document. Anyway, her business. Shall we see what is in the other envelope?"

She opened it and pulled out two high quality sheets of paper.

"Bridget, They are the title deeds to a house! It's called Coleridge Grange, in Lydney, North Devon. And the possessor is Bridget Kendall. It is dated two thousand and eleven. These must be the keys."

"What!! No!"

"Oh yes, see for yourself." She handed Bridget the deeds.

"So, Coleridge Grange was Maria's? Bequeathed to her by her mother, Eleanor. And then put in my name while Maria was still alive. I was twenty-one in two thousand and eleven. A twenty-first birthday present? It looks legal, but who is living there now, or is it empty? Maria died in October, two thousand and fifteen."

"And these envelopes have lain under this floor-board ever since," said Sandra.

"She couldn't will it to you, so she transferred it before she died. She must have taken more notice of you than you thought! And liked what she saw."

"But this is so incredible. Grandfather must have known! He doesn't seem to have said anything about it after she died. He died in February this year. Louise died of cancer in two thousand and fourteen. He wouldn't have come to England when she was ill, but why didn't he come after she died? Roger died in two thousand and thirteen. He could have come surely?"

"No idea, off-hand. There's a letter in here. It is addressed to your father. We can't open it."

"Maybe it gives some explanation," said Bridget. "This is all too much to digest right now. May I take the letters? Would you like to read them?"

"Goodness no. They are very personal. And I always prefer to know less, rather than more, when it comes to secrets."

"Very wise."

"Shall we go and have coffee now, and mull all this over? We'll take the tins down. They are yours."

"OK, thanks. Yes. Good idea."

She rang Oliver before she went home.

"Hello? Did you find anything?" he asked.

"We did. A LOT. Can you come round to my house this evening? I have made a risotto. We can have that. And may we read the letters together please?"

"Of course. I will come straight round after I leave the office shall I? I keep casual clothes here to change into."

"Lovely. See you then."

Chapter Six

Oliver arrived soon after six, and she told him the story of the search.

"Well it makes sense Bridget. You are so similar to Maria in interests, as is Richard."

"Before we look at the letters I should show you this," and she handed the Title Deeds envelope to Oliver. He whistled.

"How stunning!" he exclaimed. "So Maria was more attached to you than you thought!"

"Since she knew I was her grandchild that would be to be expected."

He read through the document carefully.

"You will have to contact these solicitors to find out what the situation at Coleridge Grange is now. Presumably these people were Maria's family solicitors."

"Yes. They must know she died."

"Yes. Since the transfer to you had been completed before she died they had no further role in its disposal."

"No. Let's look at the letters now. They should tell us a lot," she said, opening a lid. "Oh look! There's some brief attempt at a journal in this note-book. She didn't get very far......Oliver it tells the story of Richard's birth! She says, so that the truth can be known. The first entry is dated third of March, nineteen-sixty-five. I'll read it to you,

"Linden Court

3.3.1965

Mother was in her bedroom sorting out her dressing-table drawers when I arrived. I went in nervously and sat in the wicker chair.

"Mother I'm going to have a baby," I said, and she sprang round in joy.

"Oh darling!" she cried. "That is great news!"

"Not so great Mother," I said, "it's not Roger's."

"What........not Roger's?"

"No. I fell in love with his solicitor, John Kendall. It's his."

Mother sat back on her heels, grappling with all the implications.

"Does he know? Roger?" she asked. I noticed she wasn't shocked.

"No he doesn't. Aren't you angry?"

"Well....not exactly. These things happen. But I do wish you hadn't! Don't you get on with Roger? He seems to be such a lovely man." She looked at me anxiously.

"Yes he is of course. That's the problem really. He is a perfect gentleman who doesn't like to disturb his wife. We did consummate the marriage, and he does come to my room from time to time apologetically. He knows we are expected to produce an heir, but he doesn't seem to be sure exactly how to go about it. I did wonder if he might not be homosexual basically?"

"Oh dear, really?" Mother looked stricken. "And John?"

"He is a great friend of Roger's. He comes every week to play chess with him. Of course he comes on business too. Roger is looking to buy a piece of land adjoining ours but there is some dispute regarding the demarcation of the boundary line, and what is already legally ours. So all that is going on, but they are both keen chess players. So you see....."

"Yes," said Mother, "do you join in the chess?"

"Oh no. I just serve the tea and sit and watch."

"John."

"Yes, essentially. He's wonderful." I caught my breath at all that I meant by that. "He asked me to divorce Roger, but I just can't get to the point of doing that. He's too nice, and he's so kind and generous, and he just takes it for granted that people like us get married, and that's that. Plus, I mean, I have no conceivable grounds for divorcing him, and it would be such a shabby thing to drag him into the position of having to divorce me. He does make love sometimes, and seems to believe that this will produce an heir eventually. But, Mum, I'm twenty-six! And he thinks the world of John. I sometimes wonder if it might not be John he is in love with?"

"Oh gracious! Really?" exclaimed Mother, clapping her hands to her cheeks.

"Well I do think sometimes, you know, the way he looks at John. It's like we are both sitting there adoring him. "

"But darling, that's awful! I don't mean Roger's being in love with John, but for you to be in that ghastly situation! Does John realise?"

"I don't know. It isn't a subject I can bring up. He keeps coming for the chess, which you would think he wouldn't if he knew, but *even if he did, he would keep coming in order to see me wouldn't he? Maybe he doesn't suspect that. Maybe I am mistaken."*

"So what happens after the chess?" asked Mother.

"Roger takes him out to show him what he has been doing in the garden. And I tag along. I just want to be near John a bit longer, and gradually we realised we were both trying to get each other alone. In the end we were sneaking moments together in the greenhouse. It was all so sordid, but I couldn't help myself. I lived for those moments. One wonderful day we managed to kiss in the tool-shed while Roger was indoors answering the phone. John told me how much he loved me, and we arranged to meet at his house. So, in the end you see, here we are."

"Might not Roger believe the child to be his?" asked Mother unscrupulously. "He must long for an heir, and then suddenly, miraculously, here he is!"

"Mum, even he knows he has to participate, and he didn't when it was absolutely crucial that he should," I said. "I've thought through all the possible alternatives, and how, theoretically, they could play out, but in the end I know I couldn't possibly lie to Roger about a thing like this. Not possibly."

"No," agreed Mother. "You couldn't. So what are you planning to do?"

"Have it here secretly, if I may? I mean, just suppose Roger is in love with John himself? And I, his wife? I have talked to John, and told him I can't bring myself to leave Roger. I said I would have to arrange for adoption. It didn't bear thinking about, but I couldn't see any alternative. But John says he will take the baby and go away with it somewhere to bring it up. Can he? He says he can."

Oliver sat quietly in Bridget's parlour as she read out this old story, describing so vividly the situation in Ashcroft Manor at that time.

"So now we really know," said Oliver.

"Yes. Maria's Mother doesn't seem to have been all that surprised. Bit of play-acting but not devastated."

"Sounds as if her parents might have come to suspect themselves that there was something irregular about the marriage, but who was going to say anything?"

"Oh gosh Oliver! She describes here a previous scene in the old tool-shed where they must have stood among the spades and rakes. It's difficult to read out, but I will:

35

"5.12.1964

Today we sneaked, I have to say, into the tool-shed while Roger was answering the phone. We had reached crisis point really. John just launched straight into his confession,

"I am most deeply and profoundly, in love," he told me. "I can't hide it or pretend any longer. Is there any hope you might divorce Roger?"

When the moment came I found I just couldn't do this to Roger. I said something like,

"I love you too," I said, "but I love Roger in a different way, and I can't bear the thought of him having to face everyone here after such a disaster. It would destroy him. He is a dear man. How could we ever be happy? I shouldn't even be meeting you, but I can't help it."

"But it can't go on like this Maria," he said, "I have reached the point when I can't stand it any more. If we can't love each other fully I have to go away. Will you come to my cottage? Would it be possible for you to get away sometimes and meet me there?"

And so it was that we agreed that on evenings when I could visit him I would close the curtains of a bedroom facing the village, and he would know I was coming."

"Yes," said Oliver. "They were both still in their twenties."
"The early letters are in the same tin as these notes. Maria left them in order. The first is dated,

" 3.12.1965

My dearest heart,
I have delayed a day in writing to you, to allow the news from Ashcroft to reach Howick, before my letter, and you have heard about Roger's collapse.
Darling it was unbelievable. He and I had dinner as usual after our Friday chess, and then we strolled out on to the terrace. It was there Roger started to confess his feelings for me. The tragedy was that he fully believed they were reciprocated! He had fanaticised to such an extent that he thought the apparent absence of a woman in my life pointed to my being homosexual, and he had mistaken the genuine warmth of my friendship for him for passion. He told me how desperately in love he was, and he

was hoping to break it to you that your marriage could never become a real union. He then took me in his arms and started to kiss me. Oh my God.

It was only when I reacted against him rather violently that the awful truth began to dawn on him. He saw the horror in my face and sort of convulsed, and then he keeled over on to the ground. He started to sob, huge hacking sobs, and I called for James. We got him upstairs to bed and I called the doctor. I waited outside to give him some sort of account of what had happened, and then I left. We can never meet again. I have written him a letter expressing the deep friendship-love I have for him and always will, along with my grief that somehow my behaviour had led him into this very painful misunderstanding.

Darling I am so bitterly sorry about this. I know you will be devastated that he was led into such a heart-break. I blame myself for being so oblivious to anything but you, that he was able, maybe, to pick up on the passion in the air, and thought it was for him. How else could he have been so misled? There was nothing in my behaviour towards him to suggest it.

I can't begin to imagine how you will handle all this. I shall book my passage to Cape Town for as soon after Christmas as possible. I will come to Howick on December 17th and we can have Christmas together. You wanted to feed Richard yourself for at least the first three months and planned to return to Ashcroft before the New Year. Roger needs space to collect himself. Your Mother has been a Saint allowing you to present to Roger that it was she who has needed you all this time.

And now it is you yourself who has to face a terrible loss. But darling, my heart and my home will be wide open for you in Cape Town if you ever change your mind, and wish to join us. Your promises to God at the altar are now somewhat open to discussion. But on the other hand Roger loves us both. If you choose to stay with him I will make sure that you are reunited with our son whenever it proves feasible to arrange.

Until the 17th,
Your Loving John.

Oliver grimaced. "Things only got worse didn't they?"

"Yes. Another graphic account. When you said they lived on the edge you never spoke a truer word! The next letter is dated,

"18.10.1966

Dearest,
I hope you are bearing up under all that you have had to endure, and I hope Roger is well. I remember you both all the time. I will write again, a fuller letter. This letter is to let you know that I have regularised Richard's situation here."

Bridget looked up at Oliver, startled.

"I hope you will understand and forgive these embarrassingly awkward proceedings. Although I have told no-one else our history, I eventually told Louise recently. I did not tell her who Richard's real mother is of course, nor ever will without your permission. Not Louise, not anyone. She is a very kind and good lady, and one day she confided to me that she is lesbian. She has a lover, but in total secret as such a relationship is illegal. She trusted me so I trusted her with our situation. She was very brisk about it. She told me she could get Richard a local birth certificate quite easily. She went off to the registry office and confessed she had had a child illegitimately. She named me as the father. She said we were planning to get married as soon as possible. He has my surname but she is down as his mother.

The only alternative was to produce his real one you see darling. When he goes to school we must have to show one. And the "marriage"? Her mother connived with us in this, because otherwise Louise won't get married. We dressed up and went to a photographer's to have a "wedding" photograph taken. I even have a carnation in my lapel. So that is framed and in our sitting-room. We just said we got married. She now lives with me, in a separate bedroom of course, and continues to look after Richard. Her mother can hold her head up against any "insinuations".

I have bought a house on Hofmeyr Street, (same post-box), and we will move in there shortly as a regular family. For the foreseeable future this will serve. No-one is going to ask to see our marriage certificate. We have the photo up. And Richard has the birth certificate he so urgently needs. Louise is a good friend and I know you would like her. Forgive me darling. I know this must sound unspeakably awful in Cirencester. But at the coal-face needs must.

The new date of birth is 18.12.1966. It seems that in these parts a great many birth certificates don't reflect the actual date of the

38

birth, so we just fudge it along apparently. Or in our case, Louise will fudge it along. His real birth certificate must of course be retained.

In all circumstances darling, your John.

"Whew!" exclaimed Bridget." Shall we have a coffee-break now? Even just reading their history is a bit shattering."

They went into her kitchen to make coffee. Oliver stood looking out of the window as she put the kettle on.

"Wonderful view from here," he remarked. "I can imagine you standing here washing up or having a coffee, just enjoying the scene out there." Bridget smiled.

"Almost psychic of you. Yes I do. I think I bought this cottage just for the views. In fact I stand out there on the lawn a lot, just looking."

"Yes," said Oliver. "You are a person who always has time to stand and stare. Along with working hard of course. Your industry over the last few days has been vigorous!"

"Yes but one thing led to another. Sandra has given it her best. She knew Maria intimately. However, she wasn't around for her in those early years. Did Maria look for support from anyone else I wonder? Like a priest or someone. Were there Reiki healers back in the sixties?"

"I think so. She would have needed a priest with a liberal view on life! They exist, but most have quotes from the Bible."

"Oh I don't know. Give the Bible its due. Think of King David, the big hero, ancestor of Jesus, born of David's line? The writers of the Bible had a pretty cosmopolitan approach themselves."

"True, but here in East Gloucestshire? And advancement in the C of E depending on your diplomacy? Nah...Why have people turned to New Age wisdom for appreciation of the intricacies of real life?"

"Have you turned to New Age wisdom for Light?" asked Bridget shrewdly.

"Ah......you have me there. I suppose I have. I read the life of Dion Fortune. What an amazing woman! If anyone lived at the coal-face of the spirit it was she. I suppose I respond to the heroic! Not as embodied in any person, but certainly in the all-embracingness of its world-view, or in their case, cosmic-view. What's a fudged birth-certificate or two when you have a kid's life to defend? Or your woman's. Even if you are a professional upholder of the law. What of that when it comes to the crunch?"

They took their coffees into the parlour and sat on the sofa in front of the fireplace. The sofa-cover had a flowery pattern on light grey and matched one of the chairs by the window. Everything was comfy, Oliver observed. There was an eye to colour and design, and a love of natural beauty. You could sit here for ever and remain deeply comfortable. He sighed happily.

"Why the sigh?" asked Bridget with a smile.

"Oh I don't know. Satisfaction. This is such a pleasant room."

"Glad you like it. So in John's place what would you have done in a foreign land with an infant whose mother's identity you needed at all costs to conceal? Beyond certain boundaries you have to resort to a bit of jiggery-pokery probably. Whether or not the law is an ass, it has a strict view about documents."

"Do you know, this in itself points to the heart of my dissatisfaction with my own life as it is at present. Am I going to end up looking over my spectacles at clients in a quandary? Or will I know how to take the broad view and be able to accommodate the realities? Or even, I mock myself, alter the law to meet certain realities?"

"John didn't hesitate did he? He has his photo taken with a carnation in his lapel to fake a marriage with a lesbian, and allows a false birth certificate to be made citing her as his son's mum. Mind-blowing, but he is sweetly apologetic to his lover, feeling she will grasp the subtleties of his predicament. I love him!"

"And you can't confide all that to a priest because he upholds the law."

"So you bare your heart to a Reiki healer? Or someone of that ilk."

"Who will view your dilemma cosmically and comfort you that it is all contained within the great cosmogonic drama."

"What?"

"Pertaining to the cosmic approach to life! Keep up. Above petty politicking."

"Right," said Bridget. "So, basically you snap your fingers at the law when it is for your lover or your son, and cosmogonically it's all sorted?"

"Er, wait a minute. The cosmic dimension isn't lawless. We know that on the level of astro-physics. Pythagorus drew theorems, so by inference any spirituality arising from ultimate reality is governed by law."

"Karma."

"Right! If you manipulate a situation to suit yourself, but hurt someone else in the process, that is bad spirituality and there is a repercussion."

"But in the case of the false birth certificate who is hurt?" asked Bridget.

"No-one, on the face of it. John would never have done it if it had. It undermines maybe the force of the rule of law somewhere. And bear in mind, John went into this in a foreign land where he was unsure of his footing, but he was prepared to end up in jail for the sake of his loved ones. No contest when it came to them. Good spirituality? Or dodgy?" Oliver stopped to think.

"So you rise above the laws of the world if you do what you do for the sake of love? People have committed perjury and spent time in jail to protect someone. Is good spirituality sometimes bad law? That was what you were suggesting earlier."

"Yes, the purpose of law is to maintain order and mete out justice, but in some cases people are forced to make difficult decisions, and whichever way they go someone will suffer innocently. If you opt to lie you may be in a good place from the point of view of the cosmos, or you may not! But in the face of the law you are on a knife edge."

Oliver frowned in his effort to sort it out. Bridget leaned over and kissed him on the cheek.

"I love you Oliver." He looked at her quizzically.

"Is that a....... signal........as it were?"

"No. Let's get on. Next letter.

28.10.1976

How are things? I think of you so much at Ashcroft, and am comforted to know that there is so much to interest you and occupy you in your daily life. I wish I could see the botanical garden as it is now!

Richard continues to do well at Claremont. His grades are good and I very much want to send him to England to University, hopefully Bristol which would not be too far away from you for you to develop a connection with him. I enclose some snaps. He is growing tall and handsome! In a fond father's eyes.

I was interested to hear about your Reiki therapy."

Bridget paused and nodded to Oliver.

"So she was already having Reiki sessions long before Sandra's time."

"It seems to be close in concept to the holistic approach of African medicine and spirituality. The religion of South Africa is Zulu but they all share a common ground. It is an all-embracing spirituality which does not separate the physical from the spiritual. It is a way of life and everything including health, relationships, art, and death are aspects of the One. Sickness for instance is seen as the result of an imbalance in the body but that same imbalance

41

affects relationships, even with the ancestors. I was fascinated to hear that your Reiki therapist talked in almost the same way about imbalance.

My darling it pains me so very deeply to know how you suffer still. How can we ever find balance apart? I wondered if we might unite at least spiritually. May we not stand together as one, close under the great central spiritual Sun, embracing in the Light pouring down through us and around us from the Source, and channel our part of the beam to our galaxy and to our Earth? We should have specific destinations in mind, such as areas of conflict and oppression. This would be, if possible, at the same time, and in the night, say midnight for you, and one am for me, for five minutes? If one of us sleeps the other will be there, and many times we will be together.

You would have heard about the Sowetan uprising here on June 16th. Students protested against the introduction of Afrikaans as the medium of instruction in schools. The police slaughtered hundreds of those children. Desmond Tutu called Afrikaans the language of the oppressor. The march was supported by the Black Consciousness Movement. The police shot directly at the children, and Dr. Edelstein, a welfare worker, was stoned to death. Louise was very upset indeed, and we are both now activists for the anti-apartheid movement. I defend people arrested under the Group Areas Act 1966, and she holds women's meetings in our house or one of theirs. You are either for apartheid or against it. There is no neutral position.

God bless you, my darling, and bring you the balance we are both trying to achieve,

Your ever loving John.

"So by now John was an activist in the anti-apartheid cause," commented Bridget. "And here we have evidence of their spiritual sources and strength. They actually practised spiritual union! I wish I could ask Sandra about that. Maybe I can from another angle.

The next letter is dated ten years later. They were a bit sparse in their communications, weren't they, for lovers?"

"Oh I don't imagine these are all the letters," said Oliver. "These are the ones she picked out to keep. Politically significant, and giving a summary of what happened over all those years," said John. "She wanted to keep a record for whoever in the future. You, as it turns out. And there must surely have been phone calls!"

"You must be right of course." She picked up the next letter,

"10.10.1986

Dearest,

The years grind on. At least now I have the great joy of knowing you have been reunited with our son. That makes all this worthwhile, along with the services I have been able to render to the oppressed here in Cape Town. I am very much privileged to be part of this historic struggle. Nelson Mandela was offered freedom last year but he rejected it, asking what sort of freedom he was being offered when the African National Congress, the peoples' Party, was banned. There has been much violence, with the police and the army both employed in quashing resistance. Mandela is in talks constantly however, and we are not down-hearted. We will win.

I hope you and Roger keep well. You are always in my thoughts, and I long for your letters, darling. I survive on them.

I am otherwise kept pretty busy. I attended a meeting of lawyers in Durban in July. We have two major Associations of lawyers, The LHR (Lawyers for Human Rights) and the BLA (Black Lawyers Association). I am a member of the LHR and have defended many people in custody for violation of the 1966 Group Areas Act, and for Pass Law offences. These are apartheid regulations. The BLA has been concentrating more on changing the system itself. Now some of us would like to amalgamate the two bodies to make us a more powerful force for freedom, and the eventual abolition of apartheid. A man was shot in the back on his way to church last week. No reason given. Random acts of violence like these have to end. South Africa needs to become a free democratic nation including all the races. Louise too had her circle of women of all colours doing what they could to essentially create a unified front to present their demands. They meet somewhat surreptitiously in one of their houses, chosen at the last minute at random.

Otherwise there is of course my regular work at Cliffe's. We did our best to protect Richard from awareness of all the violence going on in other parts of the city. He grew up in an activists' home and is nationalist to the core, but it is wrong to allow children to become embittered about things they don't understand, and set them on a path of aggression, possibly for life. Instead we directed his attention to other more universal interests. We gave him books about European history and art. And here at the grass roots we

*showed him the wonders and beauties of the natural world. Nearly
every weekend, when possible, we drove out of the city to show him
beautiful places, or to wild life reserves. We taught him about
conservation and the need to protect our planet. We were delighted
to learn of the field trips from Bristol University to study
indigenous species here. My own consistent wish has been for him
to return to England and to you. Would that I could come too. We
sent him along to observe some dig the students were doing, and
it was a huge experience for him to be with young people from
England whose talk was not about politics. He became friendly
with Tom Hawkins, and we invited him to our house. The upshot
was that Richard became keen to apply to Bristol University
himself to do an ecology course. I was so excited I nearly betrayed
my enthusiasm. That would never have done of course. And so, he
returned to you.*

*Meanwhile we meet most nights at one a.m., my time, to unite
in channelling Light from the Source to our poor world. Sometimes
I can sense you. I dream in my imagination of one day coming to
Ashcroft myself, and spending time alone with you, but I know it
isn't going to happen. By some miracle Roger never discovered
our betrayal, and he has found contentment. You say he enjoys
Richard's visits, and now it is Richard to whom he shows his
garden! That makes me so happy. How wonderful! My heart is full
to think of that.*

Blessings and all my love, John."

"It is really painful reading all this," said Bridget. "The sheer grit and
constancy they showed to turn their lives into very positive forces for
good in their two worlds. It is an amazing story Oliver."

"Yes. Thankyou for sharing it with me Bridget. I feel very privileged."

"The next one is dated nineteen eighty-nine, and he says 'another year',
so they were writing at least yearly, around the time of Dad's real birthday.
I hope I don't end up having to break it to him that he is a year older than
he imagines!"

"18.10.1989

Dearest,
*Another year has gone by, and Richard is to join you at Ashcroft
as estate manager! I couldn't believe the wonder of it. Of course you
have made a close friend of him in the last three years, and the
conservation work you do at Ashcroft is right up his street. He*

44

sounds excited and says there will be plenty of opportunities for him to participate in other conservation and ecological projects around the country. I am so happy. With luck you will have him by you for the rest of your life. I felt so guilty having him all to myself for eighteen years, every time he did something funny or cute, wishing you had seen it, but now I am at peace. He is to have Rose Cottage he says. I wish we could visit him there but I deeply fear some mishap might occur to make Roger wonder about Richard. He does have a look of you sometimes I fear. But Roger thought I loved him. I doubt that the real truth ever crossed his mind. And to Richard Mum is Louise in Cape Town so all should be well.

And even here is there is some cause for rejoicing. De Klerk has been made leader of the National Party. He will bring about great changes in South Africa I am sure, and for the good. Louise knows him slightly. He is Afrikaaner. He is not going to pursue Botha's disastrous and evil policies. The last few years have brought about violence and hatred and huge abuses of human rights. I really believe De Klerk will usher in a new era for South Africa, and we can look for a dismantling of Group Area restrictions and eventually an abandonment of apartheid."

"The rest of this letter is missing."

"Some letters, or parts of, were too explosive, even by their standards, to keep," said Oliver. Bridget smiled.

"Anyway, time for supper. I won't call it dinner. Come through to my dining area."

She took him through to the back ground-floor room where a table was set for two.

"Sit down here, and I'll be back in a minute."

In a short time she returned with a casserole dish which she placed on one of the table-mats. Then she went back for a bowl of roast potatoes, and a plate of salad.

"Very nice," he said appreciatively. "I cook a bit myself to keep healthy, but I'm not sure I could produce anything as delicious-looking as this casserole."

"I'm not a natural cook," she said, "but I mastered a few healthy recipes to do routinely on different days, also to keep healthy."

"Where does your mother come from?" he asked.

"Her name is Beth. She was at Bristol University with Dad, in the same department, studying botany, and when he went visiting to Ashcroft Manors she went too. They bought their own car. You can imagine how she gravitated to The Botanical Garden! She even got impromptu tutorials with Maria." They got married after University. She grew up in Bath. Beth from Bath. You can trace Dad's interest in Roman Britain through her and Bath!"

"Fascinating. My parents of course were locals here. My Dad worked at Brook and Taylors and my Mother worked in the Cirencester library. They moved to Devon after Dad's retirement. That's how I have such as nice house!" She smiled. "My sister, Irene, lectures in English literature in Barnstaple. I studied law at the University College London and then joined my father's firm here in Cirencester."

"Is Irene older or younger than you?"

"Older by three years."

"Speaking of houses, I appear to have one in Lydney! I looked it up. It's near the Forest of Dean! Isn't that thrilling!"

"Yes, Coleridge Grange. After the poet no doubt?"

"Might be, but Coleridge seems to be a local name round there. I'll ring the solicitor tomorrow. Maria's mother's name was Eleanor. It was hers. You would have seen that on the Deeds. It does give me a comfortable feeling to be a woman of property. I am paying off the mortgage on this."

"Shall you keep the Grange, do you think?"

"I'll wait and see a bit. No rush decisions. I prefer to stay here because of the Arboretum, but the Forest of Dean!"

"I hope you won't leave me out of your equations. Me down there in Cape Town."

"You will be writing letters to me. You will be fine."

"I'm serious Bridget."

"No Oliver. You are going to Cape Town. I might or might not go to Lydney while you are away. I will keep you posted."

"You're angry."

"No Oliver. You have come to a realisation that you want your life to be more of a challenge. You want to fight dragons and restore order. My only query is why go to fight dragons in South Africa? What for? John did that half a century ago. They have a thriving democracy now, and I doubt they want you going there getting under their feet. We have more than enough issues right here in Briton which could use your attention. Your awakened holistic cosmogonic attention."

"You don't speak of 'woke'!"

"Heavens no! Your common-sense expertise as a solicitor channelled into the service of people in need. Something along those lines anyhow. It's your vision. And, I might suggest, taking those hypocrites by the scruffs of their necks and shoving their delicate noses into the dirt."

"Wow. Well thanks Bridget. You are the very voice of common-sense. Let me think about it."

"And you will keep me in your equation?"

"Bridget you are inextricably part of any equation of mine."

"Good. Ditto."

After the meal they returned to the parlour with a bowl of fruit and two mugs of coffee.

"Back to it," she said. "The next letter is dated,

"18.10.1996

Darling,

How are you and Roger? I get news of you both now from Richard which is such a blessing. And Bridget is growing up fast! Beth tells me she already has a little trowel in her hands, and digs. How amazing if your gift has been passed down to yet another generation! And wonderful too to think probably you inherited yours from the Greys at Howick, and that it was fostered in their arboretum. That must bring you great joy. And I feel contentment that although you missed Richard's childhood years, you can observe Bridget's. You say in your desire not to look like a proud grandmother you are actually on the reserved side with her! You could never be very reserved darling. Your smile lights up the surrounding area.

So, finally, The Truth and Reconciliation sittings are in progress. One of the Committees meets here in Cape Town so there is a lot of activity. They will go on for a long time, and it is painful to watch. We have them live on TV. I watch enough to keep informed but not enough to become obsessed.

At home we go along relatively quietly. Louise made many friends as a result of the secret meetings they used to hold, so she meets them a lot. She has time on her hands now Richard has gone, and she needs a job I think. She tells me she is waiting for the right opportunity.

I plod on at Cliffe's. I too am suffering something of the empty-nest syndrome. With Richard around there was always noise and activity in the house. I dread retirement, but my hair is going grey and I am regarded as an elder in the firm. I am not short of work, but it has become repetitive. Sometimes I am a bit bored, but I need it just to keep going.

Louise and I were never going to be best companions in isolation. As fellow-activists and fellow-parents we did great, but

47

now, aside from politics we have little to talk about. I am eternally grateful to her for rescuing Richard and me, and looking after us, so I hope not to become a drag in her old age.

How are you really darling? I picture you in your Botanical Garden, maybe shielding your eyes from the sun under a sun-hat, or plodding round in Winter wellies. I picture you in your drawing-room reading by the fire. Or out walking with Flip.

Roger is still energetic I hear from Richard. He said you both look well and he will send me some pictures.

Our nightly tryst supports me as ever. The spirit does not tire, although it is hindered sometimes by the aches or pains of the body. I hope and believe that together we have helped bring Light into the world.

Let me know if you are ever ill, or in distress, and seriously need me. In such a circumstance I would contrive to come, now that Richard is there to give me cover. I think Roger would never again want to come face to face with me, even though we share the most affectionate regard. Some things can never be forgotten. But call for me and I will come.

Love always darling, John."

Bridget looked up at Oliver.

"Whew. Things were really getting difficult by then, weren't they? He sounds tired of it all, and just wishes he could come home to Maria."

"Is there any definite proof he didn't?"

Bridget was startled.

"If it were me and I had a son now right there on the spot, I would have made it somehow."

"But then Dad and Mum would have had to be told, and he would be in hiding from Roger. Maybe they were told? They were definitely cagey that day I went to see them. But *I* was there! And he could hardly tryst with Maria under Dad's nose!"

"No, wait a minute, there was Coleridge Grange. It belonged to Maria. How easy it would have been for her to say she needed to go down to Lydney to attend to some business. Of course he would have come to Ashcroft too, to visit his son openly."

"Possibly yes. I don't remember him coming. But there is no proof he didn't. I shall be going to Lydney shortly, so I'll check round for any signs that he may have been there."

"The point to me seems to be that he had reached the stage where he hardly had the will left *not* to come, as I read him. He is desperate to be with Maria for a while before the end. He would have come. In this letter he had not yet considered the logistics, but the thought was in his mind. He was sounding her out for suggestions. What's this about the Greys of Howick?"

"Maria came from Howick. There's a house nearby belonging to the Grey family, and they have gardens and an arboretum. Google it. Sounds as if she was related to them somehow. Yes, we will definitely look into that possibility that John did come. Oh! Here we are! Listen. The next letter is dated,

15.3.2009

> *I am so excited and ecstatic to be coming to you, my darling, after all these years. Of course I was sorry to hear of the death of Sam Bairstow, but to know that I can come now to Coleridge is such very great news. His widow must be delighted to be going on a paid holiday to Torquay in May! So we shall have the Grange to ourselves for a whole month....oh my God darling.*
> *I am booking a flight to Heathrow at the end of April, and will text you the details.*
> *I have a project in mind for Bridget."*

Bridget glanced up at Oliver. What now?

> "I can't talk about this on the phone. It is a task for her if she feels she can handle it. I have an account here in Cape Town with HSBC Bank, and there is a branch in Cirencester. If I open an account there it should be fairly easy for funds to be transferred from here. I would like to open a joint-account with you in Cirencester HSBC, if you agree, to receive funds from Cape Town when the time comes later. Maybe you might be able to talk to them about it, and start the job of opening it? Then we can drive over one day and complete the business. We need the account to be on-line.*
> *My wish is to help three young people from South Africa, preferably, whose parents endured apartheid, but otherwise they must all be of African origin. This is where I would need Bridget's help if she feels up to it, to seek out and select three recipients, I suggest from deprived areas of London, for a scholarship to pay for higher education, or a vocational course, or training, or to set up a business or other scheme. The aim is to help establish them on the road to success."*

"Gosh Oliver!" Bridget looked dismayed. "How on earth?"

"Whichever of us is the survivor would be responsible for telling Bridget her history, and asking her if she feels able to take on this task. The only proviso is that Roger must not know. He would not be able to bear the pain, and could have another nervous collapse. I can't possibly do that to him a second time. If she decides to accept, the account will be transferred to her. My instinct is that Bridget is a young lady who will be able to meet this challenge. How she handles it I leave entirely up to her. How she allots the funds will have to be her decision. The amount awarded to each of the three will be different and depend on the cost of the endeavour.

We can text our comments or thoughts about this. Bridget will get the Grange and her inheritance from her father so she is provided for. My rest of my estate, held in another bank, will go to Richard.

Breathless, literally darling, with anticipation, John."

Bridget looked at Oliver dumbfounded.

"The plot just gets thicker and thicker doesn't it?" said Oliver.

"How am I expected to go trawling round the inner city schools of London talent-spotting? What was Grandfather thinking? Am I supposed to be like these TV celebrities looking for reality-show fodder?"

"Well let's wait and see if he actually followed through on his intention, but if he did you would be doing much better than that. You would be offering something real. If the time comes, you could print a few application forms and send them to the head teachers of schools in deprived areas. Ask them if there are any under-privileged youngsters in their schools who could go places with the right training? Ask them to select, say, two, and return the forms to you. Then you sift through for possibles. You can do it."

Bridget's face cleared a bit

"Put like that it does sound do-able."

"You need to find the right schools, after you receive whatever official request from Cape Town of course. I can help you with that."

"Can you? That would be really good. But by doing what?"

"I haven't thought yet, but one idea would be to ring the MPs of the poorer constituencies in London, and ask for a list of the under-achieving schools in their areas. You're looking for three teenagers, so there's no point in scouring the whole country."

"I have yet to ring that solicitor in Cape Town to ask for further enlightenment. I can ask him also now if he knows anything about this. I'll tell him I found out about it from a letter among Maria's effects."

"Good idea. We have to ask someone something. And not Richard obviously."

"We, Oliver? Are you with me in this?"

"Yeah, of course. I'll put the query-deprived of Cape Town on hold, and concentrate on the really-deprived of London for the time being. You are perfectly correct about the fool-hardiness of rushing off to Africa. It was a romantic notion prompted by comparing John's life with mine."

"Well if it's any comfort, John's life at your age wasn't enviable."

"Except for having found Maria. How many people could still be passionately in love with a woman, known for a short time, and not seen since for over fifty years? "

"Yes, the constancy was remarkable."

"Are there any more letters or papers for us to look at?"

"No. We have Dad's birth certificate, John's letters (wish we could see some of hers back), the note-book, the Title Deeds and keys, and the letter for Dad, that's it."

"And a big IT it is. You have the phone-call to Cape Town and a trip to Lydney next."

"Yes. You will come there with me won't you? I need your professional eye on things as well as your personal presence."

"About my personal presence Bridget....," he said looking at her seriously, his eyes seeking hers, "I don't want to end up like Roger, having totally misunderstood what I thought to be signals."

She looked back at him seriously.

"Like Roger? No, Oliver, like John. But we are so lucky. We don't have to snatch moments in a tool-shed. We have two houses to ourselves. Maybe even three......"

In a swift movement his arms were round her holding her so tightly she could hardly breathe.

"You love me," he murmured.

"Oh yes, Oliver, I do."

Chapter Seven

The next morning, as she stood outside on her lawn watching whisps of cloud moving gently across a pale blue sky, she decided the first thing to do today was ring Cape-Town. She must check the local time there. She and Oliver planned to go to Lydney on Saturday. She had to ring the firm which had handled the transfer of Coleridge Grange to her. Who, if anybody, was there now, and what was its condition? How amazing it would feel to be in that house where John and Maria had finally after so many years and so many trials, found time and space to come together. She felt the walls must be imprinted with the rapture. The world needed such moments in its quiver full of full of pain and anguish.

She thought with joy about the previous evening. Her whole life had been transformed since the arrival of the rosewood box containing a chess-piece and a ruby ring. She could hardly digest it all! Oliver had returned home for the night. She wasn't inviting him to her bed yet. He would be going to the office today, and they were to meet at Jesse's at six. It had become their own special place. Her mobile rang. It was Oliver.

"I just wanted to be with you a minute before I go to the office."

"Yes.... I was just thinking of John and Maria together at last in Coleridge Grange. Sort of ineffable. Reading those letters was like sharing a few seconds in their long and incredibly difficult separation. And they sacrificed their very possible happiness together to save Roger any more pain. John could just have told him it was Maria he loved and she needed a divorce. She would have got it, or even an annulment, but that was beyond the boundaries of decency to them. Roger must not be made to suffer for their happiness."

"Yes. I want to recapture for the present something of the code by which people like them lived. My bliss can never come at cost to some innocent third person. Other people do come in the way. They have to be accorded courtesy and the right to follow their own path even if accidentally, it ruins mine. I keep measuring my own values by John's. And in Cape Town he doesn't indulge in self-pity. His heart is torn by the sufferings of the black community under apartheid. His letters to his love are full of what is going on there. I wish we had all the other letters."

"And hers. She must have been following eagerly all he had to tell her about what was happening, and what he and Louise were trying to do. They even found the spirituality to unite in some sort of light-transmission into the darkness of the world! I want to follow up on that. I'll test Sandra out to see if she can point me to discovering what he meant"

"And how even it was achieved! Darling I'd better go now. I'll see you at Jesse's, and we'll continue the conversation."

After breakfast she checked the difference in time in Cape Town and found it to be one hour ahead in the Summer. So at nine o'clock she dialled the number at the top of the letter which had come with the box. After some delay a male voice said,

"Cliffe Dekker Hofmeyr, Donald Cliffe speaking."

"Hello. I am Bridget Kendall, speaking from England. You sent me a box recently containing a ring and a chess piece. They were from my grandfather, John Kendall. Thank you very much. I am ringing though to ask if you can tell me anything about them? They presented a bit of an enigma."

"It is good to speak to you Miss Kendall. John was an esteemed member of our firm for very many years, and was still in the saddle when he died from a heart-attack. We miss him a lot. Yes, I was puzzled by that box myself. John gave it to me one morning and asked me to send it to you after his death. He had just put it in an envelope with no note. He didn't explain it. He just said they were family heirlooms and you would understand. So I put it in my safe, and after his death sent it to you as requested. I take it you don't understand?"

"At first I didn't at all. After asking around I discovered the chess-piece belonged to a set at Ashcroft Manor where he used to visit a lot. So I took it back! I am assuming the ring was for me?"

"I would imagine so. They were treasures he needed to entrust to a loved-one. That's all I know."

"He didn't speak about Ashcroft Manor then?"

"No. I believe he used to make phone-calls to someone there. He would take the calls outside. Is there anything I can do for you?"

"I'm not sure. I have been left in the dark rather. Do you know anything about a bequest he made to fund the education or training of three African youngsters from deprived backgrounds here? They were preferably to be children whose parents had suffered under apartheid. Or failing that, they must be of African parents. I have learnt about this from a letter I discovered, and that I was to be charged with the responsibility of seeking out three worthy recipients, and disbursing the money as I saw fit. The thing is I have had no official notification about this. My father inherited Grandfather's estate, but there seems to have been no mention of this money, and my father seems to know nothing about it. It is important obviously to find out about it, and whether he went through with the plan. Do you have any record of it, or know who might have the instructions?"

"Oh yes, he did talk about that. It was a plan dear to his heart, and he did say he would entrust the work to a relative in England. I believe you were quite young at the time, so he had not decided who to ask. I am checking his files as we speak. Wait a minute. There is one here marked "Funding". Let me see. Yes, there is a letter addressed to you. Unfortunately he doesn't seem to have told anyone about it! That is very strange. Maybe he hesitated to send it, or thought he might edit it later, and in the end it was never put with the box. I'll post it to you, but perhaps you would like me to read it over the phone?"

"Oh yes please, Mr. Cliffe. Let me record it."

"It is a personal letter. It reads,

1.7.2016

Dearest Bridget,

When you receive this letter I shall be gone. I have so much enjoyed our talks on the phone. You are a child after my own heart, intelligent, spiritual, but with a hard core of common sense. Sweetheart I have a little task for you which I know you will like, and I hope that fulfilling it will bring you great satisfaction. My friend, Maria Featherstone, has passed away so very unexpectedly, and shortly before your twenty-fifth birthday when she was due to give you all these details herself.

I want to fund the higher education and/or vocational training and/or establishing in a business or other endeavour of the recipient's wish. There are to be three recipients selected by you from under-privileged families. They are to show exceptional talent which needs developing, or intelligence which needs education. My wish is that the recipients should be enabled to reach their full potential and take their rightful places in the world. To this end Maria and I created a joint account at the HSBC in Cirencester. Maria had the debit card and cheque-books, and the paperwork. It is an online account. It is now, sadly, in my name only, and I will soon transfer a considerable sum to that account. The amount delivered to each of the three recipients won't be equal. It must be based on requirement. I know I can rely on your wisdom in this. I think you will need to contact inner-city schools to find the sort of children I am thinking of. I would prefer all three to be children whose parents suffered under apartheid in South Africa. Failing that they must at least be children from Africa or whose parents were from Africa. I leave a lot, sweetheart to your discretion here, and don't worry if in the end you are forced to compromise on the exact credentials of the candidates. You will understand the intention here.

The bank papers must have been amongst Maria's effects, but no-one has contacted me to ask about them, so I am puzzled. It is very important that they are found. I would suggest, if the bank things can't be seen anywhere, that you look under a floor-board in the attic room containing Maria's things. It is secured with a screw. There should be biscuit tins. The contents will shock you but it is better you find them than anyone else. She may well have put the HSBC things down there too. My health now is not good, and I am quite weak. It isn't possible for me to make the journey to England, and I don't know Michael. I very much hesitate to approach him directly. If he has any doubts, or you need any assistance from this end with HSBC Cape Town, he, or you, can contact Donald Cliffe here. He is my dear friend as well as my colleague. You can tell Michael about this request, and that I have asked you to fulfil it. That will be fine, but you might feel, no doubt, all things considered, that you won't show him this letter.

I will send you keepsakes which will support your claim to be in my confidence. One actually belongs to him, so you can return it. The other will belong to you as my special gift. It was given to me, and represents more love than you can ever know. Or maybe, if you are supremely fortunate, as I was, you will come to know. There is no-one else to whom I would give it.

Much love, dear, Your Grandfather, John Kendall."

"Hello Bridget?" said Donald Cliffe, "did you get all that? I will post this letter to you now, signed delivery. I am extremely sorry I missed it. You got the box of course. Please keep me posted about the candidates you find for the money. That is very exciting, and so like John to remember the underprivileged, even after his death."

"Thank you SO much Mr. Cliffe," exclaimed Bridget. "This really clarifies everything. I hope I can find the bank things! And I hope there is some evidence that I can claim the account!"

"If you have any problem I will ring Michael myself Bridget, and ask him to help you. I can ring the bank if necessary."

"Oh will you really? Thanks a million for all this. I have been floundering badly."

She sat for a long while in her window-seat in the parlour. There was so much to take in. So much to realise. She was such a child. What did she know of the world John had inhabited? An honest and trusted lawyer, yet living on the edge, and sometimes beyond the edge, to manage the warring circumstances in his life. What had he achieved and at what cost, for all those he defended during the violence? The authorities opposed him. His credibility and reputation as a lawyer was at stake. There was so much she would never know.

But in giving her this task John had reached out to her and asked her to share a part of his world! And, in the letter, he was assuming that the truth about his relationship with Maria would have to come out. It had already. He believed she could handle it.

She texted Oliver to say Donald Cliffe had unearthed a very important letter to her from John.

The next job was to ring the Lydney solicitors who had processed the transfer of Coleridge Grange to her. The lady she spoke to said she remembered the transfer. The tenants had now both died, Mrs Bairstow around three years ago. Mrs. Featherstone had made arrangements for the house to be cleaned once a month and the cleaner had a key. He was a man called Timothy Parks, and she gave Bridget the man's mobile number. She expressed relief that Bridget Kendall had finally made an appearance!

Now she must ring Sandra. At one o'clock therefore, during the lunch-break, she gave her a call.

"Hi Bridget!" said Sandra. "Are you nearby? Come on over."

"No, I'm at home Sandra. How are you? In one of the letters in those tins John talks about a joint-account he and Maria set up at HSBC in Cirencester. It was to be transferred to me when I was twenty-five, and I was to use the money to fund three promising, intelligent, or talented under-privileged South African kids living in Britain. The money is to pay for higher education, or vocational training, and/or to set up the recipient in a business, or other career. I had no knowledge of such an account or scheme. So I put through a call to Cape Town this morning to ask John's solicitor about it."

"Sandra exclaimed, "Oh my God Bridget, how thrilling!"

"Yeah. I know. I was dismayed at first, but now I am getting quite excited really. I rang the solicitor who sent me that box, Dennis Cliffe, to ask him if he knew anything about the account. He didn't, but while we were on the line he looked in John's personal file, and found a letter to me. In it John outlines his scheme. The letter was supposed to be posted to me after his death, but Dennis Cliffe had known nothing about it. It was written after Maria's death, when John was concerned about the whereabouts of the bank stuff! Somebody should have found it, but no-one had contacted him. He suggests if it wasn't in her desk, Maria might

56

have put the HSBC stuff under a certain floor-board in her attic room! It wasn't in her desk or Michael would have found it."

"No," said Sandra. "We had to go through her desk in detail to sort out her affairs. There were no HSBC documents."

"I wondered if you might take another look under that floor-board, a bit further under? We found the tins and thought that was it. Maria was supposed to be going to talk to me herself when I was twenty-five, the age deemed mature enough by them for me to take on this task. Then she died suddenly of heart-attacks before my birthday. After she died John was in a quandary. He waited for a call from Michael, but none came. He couldn't ask him, because of course Michael wasn't up to speed on the back-ground. So July 1st the next year he wrote this letter to me, and a few months later he died. Dennis Cliffe sent me the box, but didn't even know about the letter! He read it out to me over the phone, and I recorded it. Now he is posting it."

"This story just gets more amazing," said Sandra. "Yes of course I'll search under the floor-board again, as soon as I get a chance without the children seeing. I do hope I find it. I'll ring or text immediately after the search. Will you be able to access the account?"

"I don't know. They must have planned it so that I will. Mr Cliffe says he will vouch for me, and go to HSBC Cape Town on my behalf if necessary. We'll see when or if we find the papers. There is a debit card, and cheque book, and the account is on-line."

"Right. We'll speak later after I've looked."

Bridget then rang Oliver to update him briefly, and they arranged to meet at Jesse's at six.

"I'm going to ring Donald Cliffe again. I'm puzzled about how Grandfather's letter could have been missed, and also I want to know more about his health, and what was going on with him. Louise died of cancer in two thousand and fourteen. Dad went and stayed with her the last two months of her life. Grandfather wasn't too well himself by then. People can speak cheerily on the phone when that is far from how they feel. We know he must have been devastated by Maria's death. Anyway, see you later."

"Hello again Mr. Cliffe, I'm sorry to trouble you.

I have been wondering about my Grandfather. When did he retire? When he wrote that letter you read out to me he was eighty! Was he still working? He says he was unwell. Was he sick? He died seven months later."

"No, Bridget he wasn't well," said Donald Cliffe. "You know your grandmother died of cancer in two thousand and fourteen. During her last year she was very ill and often in pain, and John looked after her at home. By then he was in his late seventies and he became very weak and tired. After her death he didn't recover as we would have liked him to. He took official retirement in two thousand and fourteen, but did come in for consultancy work from time to time. By two thousand and fifteen he was quite unwell. He walked slowly and tended to forgetfulness. That was very unlike him as his mind had always been so keen. In the end we urged him to stay at home and rest. We were worried about him driving in fact. In two thousand and sixteen he wrote that letter to you at home, and apparently asked us to pick it up and keep it here to be posted to you after his death. Since your call I have asked around here and it seems a young member of staff, an office-boy, went on his bike to get it. He says he put it on John's desk here for someone to deal with. It was in an unsealed envelope and wasn't addressed or stamped. It was just marked B. K. Seeing it lying on John's desk someone just put it in his personal file. Our personal files contain full records and details of our years of service. I wondered if he himself might have put it there. We do that sometimes when something is to be attended to later. He didn't come into the office again though, and we heard he had been diagnosed as suffering from pernicious anaemia. They weren't able to save him. He had neglected himself so badly that year, looking after your grandmother, and by two thousand and sixteen he was completely listless."

"This is so sad to hear about. You say he was forgetful. He must have thought you had the letter. Anyway there hasn't been much delay as it turns out. The box arrived only this week. I was just concerned about the background to the confusion."

"Yes, he could be vague at times those final two years. He may not have made his wishes clear to the young man who collected it. Have you found the HSBC books?"

"Not yet, thanks, but we think we know where to find them."

"Well thank goodness about that then. It was important to him."

"Yes. Let's just hope he remembered to transfer the funds! Thankyou Mr. Cliffe. I will keep you posted on what happens here."

Chapter Eight

Bridget and Oliver met at their chosen table in Jesse's at six. Oliver wore grey flannels and dark brown sweater. Bridget wore a dark blue sweater with jeans. She had put on her favourite ammonite crystal pendent and tiny silver ear-rings. She was brimming with the results of her day's phone-calls, but asked Oliver first about his day.

"Just the usual, but Michael called on Francis this morning, my partner. I don't know what's going on there. Probably nothing to do with us."

"No I'm sure it couldn't have been. Who wants his title even if Dad were eligible to make a claim? His heart is down there with the Romans in Chedworth. The idea is laughable. Let's not think about it."

"I suppose technically, if you were eligible, you might put in a claim for your son's sake," Oliver grinned.

"Ah yes, my son. I had forgotten him. John sacrificed his heart's desire so as not to hurt Roger. Would I betray him now? Anyway forget that. I have spent today in spirit with John and Maria. Let me play you the letter he wrote me July first last year. It was tucked away in the wrong file, but Dennis managed to find it when I asked. I've brought ear-phones."

Oliver concentrated seriously as he listened to Dennis Cliffe reading out John's letter. Then he looked up at Bridget.

"This is going to be quite a task isn't it? Presumably Sandra can check again under the floor-board."

"Yes, I rang to ask her to do that, and she will ring me back later."

"Hmmm. Yes. He knows now you will have to know. Shall you let on to your father?"

"I have thought about that. I now have his birth certificate. Do I just hold on to it and say nothing? I have decided yes. Maria didn't give it to him. Mum and Dad know something they aren't saying but I have no idea what."

"Maybe rumours of an affair? It is difficult to hide these things completely. There were gardeners on the estate for a start."

"Could be. Oliver, John was very unwell by the time he wrote that letter. He must have known he hadn't long. Dennis says they discovered he had pernicious anaemia. It had been undiagnosed, because of course John would just have thought he was tired."

"Oh.......that was sad."

"Yes, my grandmother had cancer and he nursed her at home through two thousand and fourteen until she died. By that time, Dennis says, he was very weak himself. He was seventy-eight after all. Then Maria died the next year. Her heart had been broken for decades. No surprises that it gave way. Dennis says John moved around slowly and was forgetful. He wanted to go didn't he? No reunions in this world. The doctors couldn't save him."

"But he had one passion left, the suffering of the African people under apartheid."

"Yes. That remained."

"So we are going to discover this account. We can always ask at the bank. And you and I together are going to fulfil his wishes," Oliver smiled at Bridget.

"We are! There is no difficulty about Coleridge Grange, by the way. Maria arranged for it to be cleaned once a month. The cleaner is Timothy Banks and he has a key. We have my key so we just go! On Saturday?"

"Wonderful. Your car or mine?"

"Yours. And Oliver we take overnight bags and return Sunday evening."

Oliver looked at her keenly.

"And we commemorate John and Maria's stay there in the appropriate way."

Bridget looked back.

"We do."

"I'm in love with you Bridget. You have my commitment."

"And you mine."

Later, before she went to bed Bridget received a phone call from Sandra saying she had indeed found the bank things. There had been bank statements and letters, a cheque book and debit card in a plastic envelope behind where the tins had been. The account was still in John's name, but Dennis Cliffe would help her sort that out. Sandra said she would drop the envelope off at Bridget's house the next day on her way to work.

At nine on Saturday morning Bridget saw Oliver's white car drawing up outside. Parking was allowed at the weekends so the next minute there was a knock at the door.

"Come in," she said, and led him through to her parlour.

"I rang up Timothy Banks. He says everything is clean and in order. The tenants vacated it before Maria died, so she asked Timothy to arrange for carpet cleaners to come in and clean all the carpets throughout. Then he had to get in decorators to decorate the whole house. It's been done in plain white, he says. It needed to be clean but I was to choose the colours myself later. There is some of Maria's own furniture there, but not much. The Bairstows' furniture was taken away. He died, and his wife stayed on for a while till she needed to go into a care home. There is a double bed of Maria's in the back bedroom, so I have bought fresh bedding for it here." She pointed to some large carry-bags. "And I also bought a set of cutlery and a few kitchen utensils. There are two arm-chairs which belonged to Maria, and a table and chairs in the dining-room. So we will manage fine."

"You've been busy," smiled Oliver. "Who is paying Timothy?"

"No-one it seems. Maria paid him up until June two thousand and sixteen. She paid him twice yearly, and the money for the first half of two thousand and sixteen had been paid before her heart attacks. So one job now is to set up a direct debit to him from me, plus arrears.

Let's put this stuff in your car."

"Shall we go via Gloucester?" asked Oliver. "It isn't very far."

The drive was very pleasant on a mid June sunny morning, and Bridget relaxed in her seat contentedly.

"I'm in a holiday mood," she said. "We must have lunch in Lydney. We definitely don't want to cook. Timothy says the oven is electric. And there is a working electric kettle."

"So all we need," said Oliver.

"I keep thinking of Maria and John coming down here. Did she meet him in Cirencester and they drove down together like this, or did he go straight there? They must have used the Bairstows' furniture, but her bed. It was so utterly romantic. They were elderly but what did they care?"

"They didn't. We don't know if John came back just the one time or whether they made a habit of it."

"No. There is still a lot to find out, if we ever do. Their first visit was in May two thousand and nine. In two thousand and twelve Louise was diagnosed with cancer. In two thousand and thirteen Roger died, but John was looking after Louise. He may have made a second trip, but not more I imagine. Mrs. Bairstow was still living in the house, and if Maria sent her off on another holiday she would have known why. The locals would have taken notice too if she had a man staying there with her a second time. You can't rule out anonymous letters to the spouse either in these situations!" As they approached Lydney Oliver said,

"We go along the High Street in the direction of Stockwell Brook. You are quiet? Not having second thoughts about me I hope?"

"Heavens no. I am a bit tensed up I suppose. I suggested to Timothy that he drop by tomorrow. We don't want to talk about the plumbing or rates today."

Coleridge Grange was a detached house set back from the main road. It had an iron gate and it was surrounded by trees. There was an air of peace about it.

They took the overnight bags upstairs and made their way through to the back bedroom where the bed was. No sooner had they put them down on the bed, than Oliver turned to her and took her in his arms.

"I'm crazy about you darling, let's just....." He drew her down on to the bed and she went unresisting.

"Oh God yes, let's just." She pulled off her dress as he removed sweater and trousers, and that was it. They rose heedlessly on a wave of passion which carried them to places they had not known existed. Afterwards the bed looked as if an earthquake had hit it.

"Oh my God darling, what was that?" cried Oliver. "I lost my mind. My body took over completely and I didn't care. The world could have stopped, people could have come in, it didn't matter. I was gone."

"Think of the energy stored in this bed, Oliver," she said, placing the palm of her hand on it.

"You mean we couldn't have raised that level of energy under our own steam?!"

"Oh yes we did. Wasn't that how, somehow, it was enhanced? No. Take no notice."

Oliver placed his hands on either side of her on the bed, and looked her straight in the eyes.

"NO Bridget. It was not. That was us. Forget them."

"Of course. You're right."

"Heavens above. We just experienced the most fabulous sex since Adam and Eve and you are attributing it to mystic intervention!"

"Maybe we should do a rerun to be sure?"

He needed no second bidding.

Later they wandered into a Starbucks with grins on their faces to order coffee and a sandwich each.

"So far, so good," commented Oliver.

"Let's look round the town and get milk and bread and whatever, and generally see what Lydney is like. Then go back to Coleridge, and come out for dinner this evening."

"Sounds good."

"It's clean and neat. We need to explore round to find if Maria left any personal things. She wasn't expecting to die so soon."

Chapter Nine

Back at the house at four o'clock they out their purchases away in the kitchen and started their exploration. There was an attic they left for later. The two front bedrooms were empty. The other back bedroom contained a chest of drawers and some book-shelves. In the top right-hand drawer there was a sealed envelope marked "Bridget". She opened it quickly.

10.10.2015

Darling Bridget,

If you are here opening this, you will know our history. You are of course my grand-daughter and I am very proud of you, as is your grandfather. This house I inherited from my mother, and transferred to your name on your twenty-first birthday.

I have no idea at present how the truth will come out. Roger was a very dear man, and I loved him too well to cause him any further hurt. Now Louise has passed away after her terrible ordeal, and your grandfather is exhausted. She suffered a great deal last year, but was very brave and patient, and Richard went there to be with her. In spite of his help John says he is not able to get over his terrible tiredness. He had booked his flight to England and then passed out at work. He was taken to hospital and the doctor warned him not to travel. I am frightened, but he says it is just anaemia. I urged him to rest and I would fly to Cape Town, but now it seems we shall not meet again on this side. I can't tell him I have had a serious heart attack, and am not expected to live. He would just come anyway.

It gave me great pleasure to see how you love the botanical garden. You have inherited "green fingers" as we used to say. John has this very fine plan for you to disburse funds from him to three worthy young African students or scholars. We set up a joint account and I was supposed to "tell all" after your twenty-fifth birthday. That was the age, we fixed on, for you to be mature enough to handle the task. John will transfer the funds on your birthday, and I was to go along with you to HSBC to hand over. Now John will have to explain things to you. I was happy to know you had developed a close understanding with him. I have taken Michael into my confidence a little. He is a good man

You have a bright future, I believe, ahead of you. I still have your father's true birth certificate. Louise was a very real mother to him, and he lacked nothing. She loved him as her son, and gave him the best of up-bringings.

It has been a strange life, and not what I had expected, but I am grateful for it all.

Your loving grand-mother, Maria.

Bridget folded the letter in her hand and looked at Oliver.

"Oliver I feel so BAD that I didn't spend more time with her! I liked her, who wouldn't? But she was so reserved I couldn't make a connection, or thought I couldn't, never realising that we were already so deeply connected all I had to do was walk with her. I'll never get over my insensitivity."

"You weren't to know Bridget. She kept you at a distance on purpose. Did you resemble her? Whatever it was, she must have had her reasons for keeping you at arm's length."

"I just feel I should have sensed something of the turmoil she must have been suffering having Dad and me right there, and never saying a word! But I never for a moment guessed."

Bridget and Oliver went down to sit in the two comfortable armchairs in the back sitting-room. Bridget held the letter in her hands and kept checking over the details.

"So, here we have it," she remarked. "At least my parents are both my parents. I am still trying to sort out their attitude. She's in love with another man, and then discovers her husband is homosexual, but she renounces the man she loves for him. And he renounces her and goes to live at the other end of the world to avoid hurting his friend, who can never be a real husband to her. I mean, what?"

"I know. I am riding that one out for the time being."

"And neither is angry or bitter. They devote themselves to their lives as they are, and don't waste them because they aren't what they wanted. She develops a botanical garden which is the pride of the county, and he takes up the cause of the black Africans under apartheid. And for God's sake sets up house with a lesbian lady to be mother to his son! And calls her Mrs. Kendall." He flopped back in his chair in awe.

"Don't forget the carnation," said Bridget. "I love that, and the photo. What an amazing woman Louise was! She went off to the authorities claiming she had had Richard illegitimately, but saying they were getting married. These were extraordinary people, Oliver. "

"They both risked their lives, and he his career, to help the cause. They could have lived comfortable lives, but she is holding clandestine meetings, and he is opposing most of his own white community, and confronting the courts with deeply controversial arguments."

"I keep wondering if I could have done it," said Bridget. "Dad used to talk about the Cape Town he grew up in. There were some award-winning conflict-photographers who called themselves the bang bang club because of course they got shot at. There were "dead zones" where violent fights took place before democratic elections. There were two quite separate societies with no contact between the two. After the peace march in Cape Town in nineteen eighty-nine bodies had to be removed. Riot police just slaughtered people. They demanded the right to peaceful demonstration, and were mown down. The white government wanted the removal of Nationalist Party at all costs. Bishop Tutu said it was the violence of the government which terrorised the people. A girl crossed an empty street and policeman just went up to her and shot her. She was sixteen years old and pregnant. De Klerk said the march was ok but he knew anyway he couldn't stop it. He said they must obey the law. What law? They had to break the apartheid laws to end them."

"Yes. When the government itself becomes a terrorist organisation enforcing unjust laws at the point of a rifle, you have to decide which side you are on. John said that. You can't sit on the fence and watch. I just feel my life is too easy. I am thirty-one, and I occupy a beautiful house given to me, furnished, by my parents. I have inherited a partnership in a solicitor's office. What have I given back? Zilch. Am I to spend my life like this comfortably on hand-me-downs, or am I to try to make a difference?"

"Well you do have these funds to help me with. That is a start."

"And even this job is a hand-me-down from John! And your funds!"

Bridget laughed, and he smiled in acknowledgement of the absurdity of his predicament.

"Listen Oliver, I agree with you, and we have decided we want to make a positive impact in our lives. As yet we don't know how, but right now we are to find three deserving deprived kids and change their lives. Doesn't matter whose idea, or whose money. We just do it, and take things from there. We are agreed. We will do things together."

Oliver looked up.

"I am so lucky to have you, and the grand-daughter of my two current heroes! I hope we can manage to do something to be proud of between us. We'll try anyway."

The next morning, Sunday, Timothy Parks arrived. He was a tall well-built man in his mid-fifties, who lived on Allaston Road. Bridget invited him in for coffee, and they stood in the kitchen to chat. Timothy asked her if she had found the letter. Lady Maria had posted it to him to leave in one of the drawers for when Bridget came.

"It's been longer than I expected," joked Timothy.

"Yes, I'm sorry about that," said Bridget. "There was a communication gap regarding this house. Still! Better late than never! We have to set up a new account with you, and pay up arrears. What about the Council Tax? It was so good of you just to keep coming after Lady Maria died."

"Oh I wasn't worried. I knew someone would come eventually. Last year the bills were paid from Cape Town, and this year Sir Michael sent a cheque."

Bridget and Oliver decided to put their belongings back in the car and go into town for some lunch. Then they would drive round the area bit, and head home. She told Timothy she would drive down regularly, and he was to phone her whenever he needed anything. She wasn't sure herself yet what she planned to do with it. Probably she would put it on rent again, she thought.

Chapter Ten

Back at home in Tavistow they relaxed over a cup of tea in the parlour.

"Shall you keep it?" asked Oliver.

"Yes I shall keep it, but it can't stay empty. I suppose I will put it up for rent. It's beautiful isn't it? That dark red brick and brown frames. Maria didn't live there either though."

"The rent would give you freedom to be unemployed for a while to pursue other goals. You wouldn't have much but it would be survival."

"True. I'll stick with the Institute for now though. I need something to show for my work there. Which reminds me I have one more week of freedom before reporting for duty"

"Could I help by calling MPs in East London to ask for advice and suggestions?"

"Oh yes, would you please? A call from a solicitor will carry some weight. I need names of which schools to approach. I will devise a simple application form to send by email to head teachers. I think three possibles from each school? I don't want or need to select from individual schools myself, and I can't deal with hundreds of applicants. Head teachers are more competent to filter out bright kids who could do something given a chance. Then I will study the applicants and choose the most worthy, on the face of it. Then interview them myself. Does that sound right?"

"Yes, except I don't think you should do the interviewing. You won't know those children at ALL! How would you discern what is really going on with them? How would you be able to judge how far what they dream of is feasible? You could be there as a neutral observer, and the less said about the money the better. They should not know about that. There could be discussion groups. They could be given topics to talk about among themselves, and you and advisers could throw in questions. Let the children talk about their ambitions to each other."

"Right," said Bridget, "that does seem to be a much wiser approach. Not paid advisers though! Grandfather's money isn't going to anybody but the children themselves. We need to know about families and the sort of help or hindrance that would come from them."

"Yes, we won't rush into this Bridget. The whole thing needs to be planned very carefully. It isn't just a question of intelligence and dreams. They need staying power, and the ability to work hard under pressure. They need courage to face adversity. They need to be likeable."

"Yes. You have thought this out so much better than I have."

"Well you have been absorbed in your family history. We just let it all simmer for a bit, and move cautiously."

"I thought I might meet Sandra tomorrow. She needs to know what is happening, and I would value her thoughts."

"Good idea, but bear in mind her husband has been visiting my partner. Don't tell her that. It is confidential, but we need to be alert to any cross-currents."

"Maria seems to have trusted her," said Bridget.

"Yes I'm sure she's all she seems to be, and the Featherstones in any case have no interests in the Kendall property. Not that they seek any, but it's just odd that Sir Michael seems to be uneasy! Or probably I am being too sensitive. He'll be checking out his insurance coverage, or something else completely different."

The next day Oliver went to work as usual, and Bridget rang Sandra. They agreed to meet for lunch. Bridget then concentrated on house-cleaning and laundry for a while. She prepared a lasagne for the evening and texted Oliver to come to her house after work. At one o'clock she met Sandra at a small cafe on Black Jack Street. They ordered coffee and a snack each, and then Sandra zoomed in, excitedly on what was the latest.

"What is Coleridge Grange like? Is it in good repair?"

"Lydney is a nice little town and it's on the outskirts. Good garden with trees. Yes it's in good repair. Maria had employed a man to look after it. John paid him last year, and Michael sent him a cheque this year. I have set up a new account with him. It was re-painted white all through to be clean, but also for me to decorate it how I like later. I would be tempted to live there but all my career goals are around here at the moment. Two front rooms, and two back rooms, ground floor, and first floor. A bed belonging to Maria is in one of the back room, and chest of drawers of hers, two arm-chairs downstairs. I took new bedding and cutlery. For overnight it was comfortable."

"So shall you rent it out then?"

"Yes I think so. It can't remain empty. How does your husband react to all this activity? Did he know or suspect that Richard was Maria's son? Does he mind?"

"I sounded him out over the weekend. He did seem to know about the affair. He doesn't know about Richard, unless there are rumours in circulation he hasn't told me about. After all, we all know his mother was South African. Why would he suspect otherwise?"

"There must have been rumours on the estate. It isn't easy to keep an affair secret."

"I imagine that's how he knew."

"And Sir Roger?"

"Oh about him being in love with John? Yes they all knew that. He had such a public melt-down. But he treated everyone well and was a kind man so it was kept hush-hush."

"So we can assume Dad is believed to be Louise's son."

"Yes. Any other idea is not admitted."

"Right."

"Between you and me and the gate-post Bridget, Ashcroft Grange was not thriving until they set up the business. Roger had the title and the house, but she had the money. It's not some great ancestral property after all. It was built in eighteen-forty, and bought by the Featherstones from the original owners before the First World War. They willed everything to Michael."

"So could the idea of an illegitimate son be uncomfortable to Michael? Surely not. If there was a will, it's his. And you know Dad. Even if he found out, he's up to his knees in that Roman Villa. Happy as a lark. He ain't going nowhere!"

"No. Theoretically, (and I don't think he does suspect Richard is Maria's son), the threat could come if you made a claim. It's a long shot, but I suppose you might. Just."

"No I mightn't Sandra. Have a heart! I've already got two houses."

"You couldn't claim the house, but with Richard's birth certificate you might, I'm not sure, be able to claim half the value in cash."

"Gosh, Sandra!" exclaimed Bridget. "No I jolly well might not!"

"It is actually far-fetched, but you asked how Michael was reacting, so I am giving you a run-down of how, theoretically in Michael's mind, things could play out."

"There was still a will Sandra."

"But you are going out with Francis Brook's partner, Oliver."

"What! Sandra? Do you really imagine I could plot with him to get half the value of your house? How do you know I'm going out with Oliver?"

"Little bird. Property is a strange thing, as John Galsworthy expounded so well in four long novels. The owning of it creates power. If you and Oliver had children?"

"Did we just fall down a rabbit-hole? Suddenly we are in Wonderland. Sandra, I promise you faithfully on Maria's grave I will never at any time make a claim on Roger and Maria's joint estate. If there is such a thing I will sign an affidavit surrendering any claim. "

"I know you won't Bridget really. Honestly. It was just that when you asked me about Michael, my thumbs pricked a bit, as if I had picked up on some worry of his."

"Well the offer of an affidavit is open."

"Right Bridget, sorry. So moving on to the account at HSBC. Are there any developments there?"

"Only that I have to go to the bank and claim it. Donald Cliffe, John's colleague in Cape Town, will help if necessary. Selecting three recipients will be a huge task. I shan't have much time either as next week I have to go back to work. The initial stages can be done by email so I can get started. Maria had left a letter for me at the Grange. She wrote it after her first heart-attack and posted it to the man who looks after the house to leave in a drawer for me. Apparently she was warned she wasn't likely to survive long. By that time Grandfather too was ailing. The plan was for her to reveal all to me after my twenty-fifth birthday. She was going to tell me who I was, transfer the account to me, and talk to me about the funding, but now she realised that probably wasn't going to be possible. She thought John would have to do it, but he was sicker than she knew. He had pernicious anaemia. It had been undiagnosed too long and he died. She didn't tell him about her heart attack because she knew he wasn't well enough to travel. Donald Cliffe said the anaemia left him very weak and a bit forgetful. Nevertheless he managed to write a good coherent letter about what he wanted done. It was supposed to be sent along with the box, but got mislaid. Donald read it over the phone to me. So here we are. I have to go to Chedworth to deliver that letter to Dad! No idea how explosive that might be, but no choice."

"Right. And you don't know what he knows either."

"They know about Roger's breakdown. I'll keep you posted, but don't worry about Natasha and Jeremy!"

"No. And in any case things unfold as they were designed to. Good luck Bridget. I'd better get back."

The next day she knew she must go to Chedworth. She had her father's birth certificate with her to give it to him. She feared some sort of show-down. Maria had left her Coleridge Grange and John had bequeathed her a job with the aid of Maria. The HSBC account was initially joint with Maria. Nothing could be concealed now. She set off. She had given her parents a call to say she was coming, so they were ready with a hot kettle when she arrived. They could tell by her face that something was up. She took a few sips of coffee and launched into the story.

"Dad, I have a letter for you from Grandfather Kendall."

Richard looked up surprised.

"Delivered by the Angel Gabriel I take it?"

"No Dad. Maria Featherstone had it. She wasn't able to give it to you because of the heart-attacks."

Richard paused and glanced at her mother.

"O.K. How did you come by it?"

"Sandra Featherstone found a tin containing papers addressed to me. I had been asking if they recognised that ring Grandfather sent me. The chess-piece was theirs. Sir Michael took me up to Maria's room where the set is kept. On her wall is a large photo of the Featherstones, and the ring is clearly to be seen on her finger. We have that smaller copy of the same photo, but you can't make out the details of the ring in ours. Sandra remembered that Maria had been taken off to hospital after her first heart-attack, and died there after a second. It occurred to her that there might be something somewhere which Maria had kept private. There were rumours, you see, and the ring was significant. She gave him her ring Dad. And he gave it to me. In the tin there was an envelope for me containing the Deeds to a house in Lydney. It was Maria's house inherited from her mother, and she had transferred it to me before she died. Along with the tin there was a folder addressed to me containing card, cheque-book and statements of an account Grandfather opened jointly with Maria in Cirencester. It was to be transferred to me by Maria after my twenty-fifth birthday to fund higher education for three African students. Then of course she died in October two thousand and fifteen, and he died early this year. I rang his colleague in Cape-Town to ask if they knew anything about the account. He checked in John's personal file and found the letter addressed to me which should have been sent with the box. Donald read it out to me over the phone and I recorded it. So that is the story Dad. Did you have any inkling of any of this?"

Her parents were speechless.

"May I hear the recording Bridget?" her father asked quietly. So she turned it on for him. Her parents listened in silence. At the end her father said,

"So Sandra's search was quite thorough!"

"Oh well, you know Dad, look under a floor-board for secrets. Doesn't need much deduction."

"Apparently not. Yes I did know about his affair with Maria. We lived on the estate all those years after all. It doesn't come as the greatest shock to learn she was my birth mother, though a lot of ingenuity must have gone into the deception. And the mother I shall always regard as my real mother had to have helped."

"She seems to have been a lady of great resourcefulness Dad."

"She was indeed. The stories I could tell about her! So when was I really born? Break it gently."

"October eighteenth, nineteen-sixty-five. Not too bad. This is your original birth-certificate, but your South African one is your official birth certificate."

She handed him the envelope, and he took it out warily. After he and her mother had studied every detail of it she said,

"And Dad, there is a letter from Grandfather addressed to you."

She handed him the envelope addressed to him in his father's writing.

"Oh hell. OK, my mother was not my mum, but I don't want any maudlin explanations. You read it and judge if I can stand it."

He handed her back the envelope.

"Dad, Grandfather wasn't sentimental. He was a fighter! He did what he believed he had to do, and of course it is hard to swallow now, but he isn't going to slop over you is he?"

"You check it through anyway, and if it isn't going to be palatable to me please keep it yourself."

"OK. Give me a minute."

In fact, knowing her Grandfather's letters as well as she did, she was a tad apprehensive. However he knew his son, and had of course understood what his chief concern was going to be. It read,

My dear Richard,

When you read this I shall have gone. Imminent as my departure seems likely to be, I find it difficult to imagine you reading this without me there to interrupt all the time. I have been diagnosed with pernicious anaemia, too advanced to mend. I was not at all well of course when you were here, but then I just thought I was tired.

I have delayed any reveal-all talk with you because I did not want to change our world or our father-son dynamic. Our home-life in Cape Town was such fun, and so exciting, I believe you could hardly have had a happier childhood, and that in spite of the violence of the apartheid back-ground. And who made every day an adventure, and made us laugh, and feel so comfortable with ourselves? Your Mum. She was a wonderful woman.

You know of course that her father worked at Cliffe's, and that I arrived in Cape Town after his death when Louise was looking for a job. Learning that I was a single parent, Cliffe's recommended her to me as home-help cum nanny. She was educated, intelligent, a natural home-maker, and funny. She and I became comrades, and even at times, bordering on, comrades-at-arms. In spite of her privileged white background, she took up the black African cause with zeal and tenacity, completely fearless, and with skilled leadership. She and the friends she gathered around her worked constantly to undermine the grip apartheid had on the common people. Yet, in spite of all she was doing in the city, she maintained our home as a safe zone for a growing boy.

She was always full of ideas for expeditions or activities, and she always the best fun. I therefore do not want you to imagine that at any stage I under-appreciated her. Who could? She was a force of nature, as they say. But you would have realised later, looking back, that we were not lovers. We did not share the same bedroom, and there were none of the husband-wifely spats or jokes. We were mates. Best friends. We came up with the plan in my second year in Cape Town of becoming a family. She sorted out the hitch that you needed a new birth certificate, and she attended to your school admission. She was a local, and knew how to handle the authorities. I had no secrets from her, Richard, nor she from me, except that I did not name your birth mother to anyone. Our arrangement suited both of us. And it worked.

As to your birth mother, I don't believe I need to spell out much. You came to know Maria and Roger so well that I don't have to discuss them, or apologise for anyone. In those days I had no notion of leaving England. You were born in Northumberland, and Eleanor, Maria's mother, looked after her. They were connected with the Grays of Howick, and I have always believed that Maria's powerful gift in plant rearing was inherited from them. She spent much of her childhood in their arboretum learning the skills she used later so advantageously in the botanical garden. Even you and Bridget have inherited that gift.

I have made arrangements for Bridget, if she is willing to take on the task, to allocate funds I shall transfer to an account in HSBC Cirencester, to three deserving students or scholars whose parents were originally from South Africa. My first preference is that their parents should have suffered under apartheid. The instruction is not hard and fast however, but the recipients must be of African descent, and preferably South African, I have talked with Bridget enough on the phone to feel she is up to this challenge, and through fulfilling it will share something of the awareness we attained during those years. The eyes are opened and I want that for Bridget.

It was wonderful to have you with us during those final terrible months for Louise..

Your loving father, John Kendall.

"Dad," said Bridget, "this is a lovely letter. Nothing at ALL soppy! Read it," and she handed it to him.

He took it and read it, and then passed it to her mother.

"Yes...," he said. "I did get to hear the rumours at Ashcroft of course, but played deaf. I picked up on the implications too. That story about Roger everyone knew. There was no real evidence about her that I could tell. Father was in Cape Town from nineteen sixty-six and I had proof I thought, that I was born there. So I treated the gossip as just talk. Then Father came to visit us in two thousand and nine. He said he had come on business, and just spent a week with us. He never went near the Manor. He asked me if I had heard the Roger story, which of course I had, and said he was concealing his visit so as to avoid meeting Roger. I completely understood, but I felt bound to mention the other story in circulation that he had an affair with Lady Maria. From his response I could see it was probably true. I left it at that. After all it all happened well before he met Mum."

"What did you think when I showed you the chess-piece and the ring?"

"The obvious of course, that he had keepsakes from her, and, probably, him. I might have felt angry, but when Mum was dying he never left her. He kept her company through the night, and shared the daytime jobs with me. No husband could have done more. So I knew he didn't regard her as second-best, no matter what had happened in the past."

Her mother put the letter on the table.

"Have you asked about this account at the bank? Shall you take on the job?"

"No I'm going to the bank tomorrow. I have a friend who is also my solicitor, so he will go with me, and Donald Cliffe is on call. Dad, I was thinking, my friend, Oliver Taylor, says I must have advice on who to select. I have no direct knowledge of east London, and none about the African community. Would you, when the time comes, be willing to go there with me to help me vet the candidates. Oliver says no mention should be made of the money, and he suggests holding group discussions of the children themselves talking about their ambitions. They would have to be arranged in one of the schools. Of course head-teachers would know what they were about. I am going to contact head teachers of inner city schools and ask them to select three from their own schools. Then get them all together. Will you come? You can even surprise them with your Xhosa! Get them to talk!"

Her father was excited at the idea.

"Probably they won't speak it! It will all be east London dialect now, but yes I would love to come! Thanks for asking! It will be such a great experience to meet kids from my own back-ground."

"And probably it will be you telling them about their back-ground. Could we even make meeting you the justification for the get-together?"

"If you like, and serve with bunny chow and coke!"

"What on earth is bunny chow?" she asked.

"A South African burger. I think you can buy them in London now."

"Oh, definitely bunny chow then. That should loosen their tongues! I need them relaxed and talking. I'm starting to look forward to this myself now. With you I can handle it."

Richard started to talk about his childhood in Cape Town, and Bridget was enthralled to realise how vivid those years were still in his memory.

"We'll go sometime Bridget, you and mum and me, and I'll show you all the old haunts!"

"Dad, I'd love it!"

Chapter Eleven

Oliver arrived at six-thirty after having been home to change.

"I've missed you," he murmured, holding her tight. "After a wonderful weekend being together all the time it has been so lonely."

"Stay the night."

"I will."

"Stay many nights."

"I will. You mean move in?"

"We've got three houses. Which one?"

"These two during the week, and Lydney at the weekends."

"Like the mad hatter's tea-party. Sounds like a plan."

"How did things go in Chedworth?"

She told him what had happened.

"I didn't tell about the letters from Grandfather. No way were they ever meant for him to see, and as it turned out he was hesitant even to read his own in case it might be 'maudlin'. I had to look at it first to check on its' tone before he was prepared to read it. It was a very good letter talking about Louise, and moving on to the African children. He said very little about Maria. Dad heard what they used to say on the Ashcroft estate about an affair, and already knew there was speculation about his parentage. So he wasn't shattered. Grandfather knew that by the time he got his letter Dad must have heard the truth, so he didn't sentimentalise. Oliver, I asked Dad if he would be my adviser in the selection of the children. It makes total sense. He even speaks Xsosa which they probably won't. We sketched out the idea of inviting them ostensibly to meet Dad, and enjoy a sort of South Africa Fest with bunny chows, which to the uninitiated are South African burgers, and cokes. Talk about the homeland, how things are going here, hopes for the future. There would be no mention of money. And Dad would be able to assess the children and gauge what they have in them to develop. No system of assessment can be fool-proof, but I think this way we have the best chance. And he is from outside. He has no personal interest in any child himself. And we would need you to be there, Oliver and Mum. We want the children to be relaxed and chatty. What do you think?"

"It sounds splendid, if we could bring about such a thing," said Oliver. "So no wobblies?"

"Not at all. In any case he tends more to the stiff upper lip. Grandfather had visited them in two thousand and nine at Ashcroft, the time when he came to be with Maria at Lydney. Dad said he went nowhere near the Manor, because, he explained, of not wanting to face Roger. Dad mentioned the rumours about him and Maria, and gathered from his response that they were true, but that was long before he met Louise. He said Dad looked after her night and day during the cancer so he exonerated him from possibly treating her as second-best. He realises now from the letter that she too had something of a past, and they had made a pact. He had guessed the ring must be from Maria, and the chess-piece from Roger."

Oliver thought it over a while, leaning forward in his chair and clasping his hands.

"Alright, good. I took the liberty of going to HSBC today to ask about the mechanics of transferring your account. They checked out the details on their computer and found he named you as his nominee. They were informed about Maria's death. Who did that? Francis? So you need to produce your birth certificate, and utility bills of course, and a copy of John's death certificate which presumably you can get from your father."

"Oh thanks, that's great Oliver. My time is running out, and I still have a lot to do. I have to think about my letter to head-teachers, and a form to be filled in."

"Oh yes, and I have looked up east London constituencies, which for want of anything better, we were treating as our target area."

"Oh, fantastic. How many are there?"

"About five, but in fact, it turns out, South Africans are not to be found much in those poorer areas, Bridget. Rather, I discovered they are to be found mainly in Wimbledon, Earlsfield, and Southfields, and by the looks of it these are not deprived people! There is an Africa Centre which runs art, music film, theatre, and literature events. There's the Wandle Pub in Earlsfield which is a hub for South Africans round there, and they can drop in to watch the Springboks. There's something called Black Pepper which provides entertainment especially for South Africans and they have a newspaper called The South African Times, the voice of South Africa. In the deprived constituencies of east London you get Nigerians but mainly other ethnicities. We're going to have to think again Bridget, and talk to your father. The South African scene in London doesn't seem to be what John imagined. Of course there are other deprived people in those constituencies . Poplar, parts of the Isle of Dogs, Hackney, East Ham have high deprivation figures."

Bridget was dismayed.

"Gosh Oliver!"

"Yeah. No poor South Africans? Now what do we do?" he laughed. "Never mind. Your Dad sounds enthusiastic. Let's ask him if he can suggest where to look for three poor kids."

"We are going to have to rethink this. If the South African community is affluent they have the means to help their own people."

"I checked for the most deprived constituencies in London generally, and Hackney comes first, followed by Haringey. After them Kensington and Chelsea if you can believe it, but I feel they should be allowed to look after their own. "

"So we could check out Hackney and Haringey and find how many of any sort of Africans there are there."

"Yes we can do that. This is as far as I have got so far."

"Well done Oliver. This is a huge step in the right direction. Should we ring their Councils?"

"Not sure. There's many an unscrupulous councillor. I would need a pretext. Like my son's school project. Don't let those greedy Councils get wind of any funding. Let me tackle this. If necessary I will say I am a solicitor looking into something, which I am of course."

"We can google secondary schools in the two boroughs can't we?"

"Yes, we'll do that to see how many there are and where. Any direct approach to a school would have to be your emails, asking something-something in a general way. Any school which has African pupils can be sent your form. The early stages have to be very cautious. I could ring up a few solicitors if you like, being frank, confidentially, about what is going on."

"Sounds good, Oliver. Please feel free to make whatever approaches you think would be helpful. Why don't we have supper now?"

They went through to her dining-room where she had already laid the table, and she went to bring the lasagne from the kitchen.

"Mmmmm wonderful smell," he said appreciatively. "It is good to sit down to a home-cooked meal. I do cook, and leave things prepared, but not often enough."

"How often do you see your family?"

"Fairly regularly. They aren't too far away. Probably every month."

"Is your sister married?"

"Irene, yes. She has a baby daughter, Juliet. My parents don't live too far away from her so they get to visit quite often."

"Would you like to have children?"

He grinned.

"If the lady is prepared to trust me with them."

"Oh, I'm sure the lady would."

"So, let's get to know each other. We can start by naming our three favourite classical composers, our three favourite pop songs, Our three favourite classical novelists, and our three favourite modern novelists, and our favourite gallery in the National Gallery, just off the tops of our heads, not our deep considered opinions. Are you ready?"

"Yes."

"Three favourite classical composers, you first."

"Mozart, Chopin, Debussey"

"Mozart, Beethoven, Bach Three favourite pop songs?"

"Let it Be, I will always love you, Circle of Life."

"Black or White, Imagine, Shotgun. Classical novelists?"

"Jane Austen, Emily Bronte, Charlotte Bronte."

"Charles Dickens, Tolstoy, Anthony Trollope. Modern novelists?"

"Phil Rickman, Len Deighton, Laini Taylor."

"Robert Masello, Frederick Forsyth, Ellis Peters. Which gallery?"

"Flemish."

"Impressionists. So, summing up, we could go to concerts together, read each others' books, and go to art galleries together. Who's Laini Taylor?"

"She writes adult fantasy stories. I got hooked on "Daughter of Smoke and Bone" about an art student called Karou. Where she lives is a secret because she was brought up by and lives with fantastical creatures who are partly human and partly animal. They need teeth to exchange for wishes. She meets up with a seraph called Akiva, and the fantastical creatures are ancient enemies of the Seraphim. It's a trilogy and complicated, but I love it. Whose Robert Masello?"

"Well he too writes fantasy, but more supernatural fantasy. His books are about good versus evil. Ancient relics are discovered which have hidden power, and there will be a race to get possession of them to destroy them or harness them. Lots of mystery and thrill!"

"Sounds exciting. I must try one."

"So shall we move in together, in any of our houses?"

"No. We need to get to know each other much better first. A person you live with can drive you crazy because of some silly trick like a snort, or using some phrase repetitively. We need to identify traits which could drive us mad before we actually try to live with it. We need to know what to expect of each other, and what not to expect of each other. So many things."

"Bridget I don't snort! Nor do I cough or hiccup un-necessarily. I don't slurp or grab the best chair. I was nicely brought up. And you were brought up superbly."

"Thankyou. I know. I just think that for some time to come we need to be able to return to one of our own houses to recuperate quietly from the adjustment process, and there always is a period of adjustment when you start to live with someone Oliver."

Oliver pondered.

"You're not wrong. I just miss you when I'm at home alone."

"Well that's good. I miss you too. That will help us get used to each other's full-time presence, less work, when we do live together."

"So you do see it as 'when' Bridget?"

"Oh yes, definitely."

"What do you like to do that you feel might become difficult if you live with somebody?"

"Well, first thing in the morning I like to stand outside, or stand looking outside, quietly looking at things. It isn't exactly meditation so much as contemplation. I sort of absorb the vibes f the natural world for awhile, with a mug of coffee. After that I feel ready to face the world."

"Right, I will remember."

"And no watching me from the window. I have to be left alone. What about you? What do you need?"

"Something a bit the same actually, but at the other end of the day. I like to come in from work and flop in an armchair with a coffee, and just relax. I let the affairs of the day slip away for about half an hour. No talking. Just peace."

"And you shall have it. Do you prefer to make your own coffee?"

"Oh definitely. I've gone into silent mode."

"So those are two things we know about each other straight away! I'll do a bit of shopping or something while you unwind." She smiled.

They put their dishes in her washing machine and went back to the parlour. Then sat together on the sofa in each others' arms.

"I love you so much Bridget," he whispered pulling down the zip of her dress. She pulled off his sweater and gripped his body in her hands feeling its' contours and nuzzling into his neck. He shivered and gasped.

"Oh my God darling... I'm going crazy. Bed!"

"They spent a long time exploring each other thoroughly, crying out with pleasure until the climax."

"It was hard for me getting through today thinking of this," panted Oliver.

"Concentrating on funding and all that."

"A passionate love affair is an end in itself. It's difficult turning one's attention to other matters, however important."

"You feel that too do you? And just the thought of John and Maria!"

"I know! I just want to grab you but have to be civilised," groaned Oliver.

"Well no more civilisation for tonight. We can let it all out for once...."

Chapter Twelve

The next morning Oliver accompanied her to the bank before going on to his office. Bridget rang her father early and asked him to scan and email John's death certificate, and there was no difficulty setting up the account in her name. She was stunned to discover it held just over a hundred thousand pounds.

"A hundred thousand Oliver!" she exclaimed. "This is a huge responsibility! We've got to get it right. I'll start composing letters to head teachers. Then there will be time to edit and correct it several times before sending it."

"I'll contact a couple of solicitor acquaintances in London first. But it isn't all that much in fact Bridget. It costs two hundred thousand to make one doctor. We are going to have to put a lot of thought into this. I'll ring you."

She returned home dismayed to find herself responsible for so large a sum, and despondent to realise that it could nowhere near meet the astronomical costs nowadays of a professional training. Not times three it couldn't. And to meet the astronomical costs there were already loans available now. NHS offered a bursary but what you were given depended on what you already had. She could not use her money effectively to subsidise the NHS. University was hugely expensive but for that too government loans were available. An advantage of selecting London children was that any training could be done in London and they could live at home.

At home she took out her laptop to browse. She discovered there was any number of schemes already in place to help the under-privileged. Several charities already offered tuitions and support. There was Urban Synergy which helped children from eleven to eighteen to reach their potential, Access UK which provided career support for minority youth aged sixteen to thirty, the Reach Society to motivate and inspire black boys and young men, Westside Young Leaders Academy to instil the tenets of success at an early age, the Eastside Young Leaders Academy to enable students especially black and minority ethnic boys to become transformational leaders and global citizens, the Southside Young Leaders Academy to assist in personal development and inspire boys to be agents of change in their own lives, The National Association of Black Supplementary Schools to provide supplementary schooling to black children, the Super You Academy to help those with poor self-esteem,

African Sons and Daughters to develop the social, economical, and physical well-being of the African community in the UK and the world-wide African Diaspora, the Black Child Agenda to help stop black children ending up in prison, Ultra Education to ensure that all children of African, Asian, and Caribbean heritage to proactively engage with their psychological lives, Father2Father to support and mentor adolescent boys, and even something called The Gentlemen's Network to assist males through the transition from boyhood to manhood!! And these were not all. There were numerous schemes already in place to provide individual tuition to minority children.

What corner of African or Asian or Caribbean childhood had not already been exhaustively addressed? Her grandfather's hundred thousand began to look rather sad. There seemed to be literally nowhere to put it. Yesterday they had been so excited and full of plans, and now she realised they were all utterly superfluous to requirement.

She jotted down the names of the agencies already in place to show Oliver and closed her laptop. All students who attained the necessary grades could apply to universities and get loans they may never repay. Colour was neither here nor there. Anyway, worrying about a spare hundred thousand pounds in one's account didn't make sense, and Grandfather had in the end left the use of it to her discretion. The recipients had to be of African descent though.

Oliver rang her at lunch-time. He had a rung his contact in London, Jim Slater, and Jim had been very doubtful about an individual trying to fund students outside the system. There were charities she could pay the money into

"He's right Oliver," she said. "I've spent most of the morning trying to find out about the situation with poor black African pupils and flagged up umpteen agencies already involved in the support and advancement of young black people. In one place alone there was a list of twenty-five organisations working to assist the black community. I listed I think thirteen specialising in extra classes and tuitions for black pupils, and once they have achieved the necessary marks they can apply to universities like anyone else. I am stumped for the moment. I'll ring Dad."

She made an omelette for lunch and rang Richard. He was disappointed that they could not apparently look forward to a South Africa jamboree, but said he would think about it.

It didn't make sense. There was so much media talk about deprivation and poor standards amongst Africans in schools and their lack of opportunities, and yet on the internet there were all these photos of bright intelligent young black students smiling and laughing and looking well-fed, and apparently fulfilling their dreams. She sighed. She felt like a do-gooder on the prowl for some poor, and disappointed everybody seemed fine! She could always ask the Archbishop of Canterbury. He seemed to have a hot line to the needy. Nah.

She was going to Oliver's house this evening with an overnight bag. She turned on the internet and began to scroll comprehensive schools in London. Then her mobile rang again. It was her Dad.

"Bridget I've visualised a possible scenario. It might be totally daft and unworkable, and don't hesitate to say so if it is, but I wondered if we might approach this from a different angle. I'm this elderly Anglo-Dutch guy who grew up in Cape Town right? I witnessed first-hand the struggles of apartheid, but I reminisce about my happy childhood there. I want to invite South African children, or children of South African parents to wherever for a get-together. It is to be a South Africa Fest. A few flags and lots of photos as props, and a South African lunch. I give a little talk about my memories, but they are free to butt in with questions and comments. It all has to be relaxed. After the talk we mingle and I try to chat with as many as possible. I shall be trying to sound them out about how they are doing in London. What jobs do their parents have. How many have Dads. The drug scene and knife crime where they live in London and how they affect their lives and their education. Buffet lunch still chatting. You and Olive and Mum as well. And just see if our antennae can pick up on any real distress. To the head teachers it has to look educational. What do you think?" Bridget was speechless for a moment.

"Dad, it sounds just fabulous. It has to be genuine fun. Pop music. Bits of video. You are brilliant. Thanks. This sounds like something we can work on."

"And even if they are well fed, well educated, and generally thriving it will still be a party won't it? I have to take the talk seriously, but I can work something out. How about the South African High Commissioner as Chief Guest? No. He would steal the show. The show is the children. Anyway something to think about."

"Thanks Dad really. It sounds amazing."

Chapter Thirteen

She arrived at Oliver's house at seven o'clock and was invited into his rather more sumptuous drawing-room, and showed her to the sofa. The sofa and arm-chairs were covered in heavy brown velvety cloth. The carpet was pale fawn. The fire-place was grey-white marble and a gold metal carriage style clock stood in the middle. To either side were china figurines and a framed photo of his parents. A walnut cabinet stood against the wall by the door. It had cupboards below and shelves above with china and other ornaments on them. The satiny curtains covering the window opposite were of a gold and cream design. Behind their sofa was an oak sideboard with a lace cover and a vase of flowers and a bowl of fruit on it. It looked like one's parents' house! She smiled.

"What?" asked Oliver.

"Nothing," she said.

"The house," he guessed. "You can make alterations."

"No!" she was shocked. "It's beautiful. And I'm like Sandra in that. I don't move into a place to give it a make-over. I enjoy its' history and its' own ambience. Your Mum took a lot of pride in this, and, supposing, I live here, like a third of my time, I shall just enjoy it."

"Mum is going to love you. You will even allow her carriage clock to stay?"

"If it allows me to stay. Oliver I don't have any rights over you or your possessions. I suppose marriage allocates rights, and I'm not sure I agree with marriage."

"Well I do!" cried Oliver.

"You are a lawyer. It is your role in life to apportion rights and property." She grinned.

"But between you and me it's your clock so I love it."

"You won't say that about all my possessions I can guarantee."

"Well ditto I suppose. But I shall be polite I hope."

"I'm trying not to allow my heart to become the heart of a lawyer. This is what I'm working on right now. That fake birth certificate. I want to be able to shove the law aside like that when it clashes with love."

"Though the law is meant to intervene to see that justice is done when people are at war over their respective loves"

"You should have been a lawyer."

"Never!"

"Why do you say it like that? I'm a lawyer, so you are, taking the analogy of the carriage clock, going to give the law the home I gave it in my environment."

"Yes of course. I am law-abiding in any case."

"But you like to stand outside first thing in the morning for a while gazing at the clouds and setting your inner compass."

"So I gather your Dad thought of a way through or round our funding impasse?"

"Yes, and I think it's a winner. We need to let this idea simmer a bit too to discover if there are any snags. We throw a party."

Oliver's eye-brows went up.

"Sounds good. You mean you and I will? Who's coming?"

"Ostensibly Dad will. And the guests are to be young people from South Africa, or the children of South African parents. He, an Anglo-Dutch grandfather, in his old age, is drowning in nostalgia for the Cape Town of his childhood. He wants to meet up with his clan and talk Xhosa or Cape Town English with them, (not Dutch, though he speaks it), and share old snaps, and have a real old-time South African lunch. We'll put on music and videos, and it really will be a party. He can do it. He has charisma, based probably on the feeling of entitlement his white skin gave him without his even realising it. It gave him presence. We are to try to round up suitable children from around, hopefully, the Hackney area, and invite ourselves to a secondary school there on the pretext that this is going to be educational. Dad will give a talk about apartheid and what it was like living with it. He will try to strike chords in the minds of these children living in racist London. The children will be free to interrupt to say whatever they want, and we shall all mingle. He will try to talk to as many as possible, and suss out any kids with issues. You and Mum and I will help. And he will order the genuine lunch."

"I am stunned! I have lived in way too small a pool. Such a scheme wouldn't have occurred to me in a thousand years. I'd be having little consultations with colleagues and teachers, and weighing odds for ever. Your Dad thinks of a party."

"Yes he considered inviting the South African High Commissioner, which he was perfectly ready to do, but decided against it because the HC might upstage the kids. He would of course and there'd be the entourage. The occasion is to be strictly child-centred. What do you think? Does your lawyer's mind detect any snags? He's waiting to hear any. He is not at all gung-ho about it."

"He thinks big. I need to talk to him and see if I can't get some of his glamour to rub off on to me."

"Darling you disparage yourself. I like you just as you are, squashing my flights of fancy, and looking at me steadily when I'm trying to flap my wings. Mum is steady. You'll see."

"Thanks. But seriously I can't see any basic snag, beyond foisting our party on to a school, and corralling twenty to thirty guests into our fold."

"Yes. These are challenges, but we'll plan out our strategy. What do we have to lose?" said Bridget.

"Nothing I guess. I'm getting this light-headed feeling. Is my name Oliver Taylor? I believe so. Is this the same Oliver Taylor who is planning a party for a bunch of South African kids whose names he doesn't know yet in a school yet to be selected and approached? That will be the guy. A dynamic passionate type always looking for the next amazing exploit? Nah."

"You mean you are experiencing an identity crisis," said Bridget.

"It's meeting you. Ever since you walked into my office life has been a roller-coaster and I'm not sure which way up is the ground."

She laughed.

"OK. So what's for supper?"

"Ah. Thanks. Yes. I've cooked a Chinese meal. Someone gave me a Chinese recipe book so I have given it a go. You just put the vegs in a wok and toss them around and add the noodles. It smells good."

"When shall we have it?"

"Now?" He took her through to his dining-room and watched her face.

"You can laugh if you like."

He had a mahogany coloured table for six chairs, all with carved legs. The chairs had velvet-covered dark brown seats. Two places were set with crisp white napkins and silver cutlery. Heavy green brocaded curtains were draw across the window. A Victoria side-board stood against a wall.

"It's hard to breathe isn't it?" he commented.

"It's beautiful Oliver, really. Relax!"

"You sit there. I left it in the oven to keep warm."

He brought in a green ceramic bowl full of the chow mein, and then went back to bring a plate of spring rolls.

"I bought these."

"Delicious," she said.

It was comfortable and secure sitting in his dining-room. The struggles of the modern world seemed far away. He had put on light music, and she felt utterly happy.

"There's a lot to be said for stability," she remarked. "I would never embark on an adventure just for the sake of it. I do like to be comfortable."

"So do I normally, but we need to have adventures to look back on Bridget. And in fact I'm looking forward to this party. It will be fun meeting London school children, and hearing about their view of the world. Very different from Gloucestershire I imagine."

"Let's video-call Dad after supper," she suggested.

"Good idea."

They took coffee into the drawing-room and Bridget put a video call through to her parents. Her father took the call, realising that she would want to discuss the party.

"Hi Bridget, have you given any more thought to what we were talking about?"

"Yes Dad, I'm here with Oliver who is one of the team, or team-leader, being our legal advisor. We are both on board for the party. Now we have to browse schools."

"No we don't Bridget. I have been studying Hackney secondary schools myself, and if you allow me to put forward my suggestion I can save you a lot of hard work."

Bridget looked at Oliver.

"What is your suggestion Dad?"

"The Butler Memorial School in central Hackney. It is funded jointly by the C of E, Diocese of London, and the Borough of Hackney. It is co-educational for children from eleven to nineteen. It offers GCSEs, BTECs, and ASDAN awards, and the option to study from a range of A levels. 11-19. They organised a trip to South Africa last year! It also specialises in sports. Ofsted rating outstanding. However under-privileged some of the children are we need good standards in the school. And last but not least we need a good venue for our bash. What do you say?"

"Butler?" asked Oliver.

"Josephine Butler, social reformer of the nineteenth century."

"What do you think Oliver?" asked Bridget.

"And presumably they have plenty of African-origin students?" said Oliver.

"Middle of Hackney? Of course. And we are looking for bright children, children with potential, so the school mustn't be mediocre. It has to be able to deliver."

"If Bridget is in agreement it sounds good to me. We are looking for a venue to which children from the neighbouring schools can go, so that too must be smart."

"Fine by me," said Bridget. "Dad shall you contact them since it is you who have the nostalgia, etc."

"Yes. I have to think that out yet."

"Right Dad."

"Bridget," said her mother. "This all sounds very exciting. May we meet Oliver properly?"

Bridget handed her phone to Oliver.

"My Mum, Beth Kendall."

"Hello, Mrs. Kendall, I am very pleased to meet you."

"Hello Oliver. You both have already been working hard on all this. Who would have thought when Bridget received that box in the post last week, that it would lead to all this? John and Louise used to ring every month so I got to know them quite well."

"Yes, I am wishing I could have met them myself. They were special people."

"They were indeed, and far too busy to write their autobiographies like so many seem able to do now even in their twenties."

"It's all big business now Mrs. Kendall, like being on twitter. Everyone is trying to promote his or her brand."

"Not 'his or her' I think Oliver. 'His' has been replaced by the plural 'their'," remarked Beth.

Oliver laughed.

"True. I have been bowled over by the stories of their exploits. We need to do John justice here. Turns out there are more than enough charities and schemes already in place to aid students of African plus under-privileged backgrounds. We needed something to target a very few individuals. A party is unconventional but so was John. What a pity we can't have them at our jamboree! We need music. Can you organise that too Richard? The real authentic Xhosa sound?"

"Of course. I have CDs."

"Fantastic. Right, so that too is sorted. How do you intend to approach the head teacher?"

"I'm still working on that, Oliver. I'll write formally on paper first, and suggest a meeting. I would need to go up to London personally in any case, to initiate things."

"You mean, to lay on the charm, Dad," clarified Bridget.

"That too of course, There's nothing like the personal touch."

"Shall I come with you?" asked Bridget.

"Heavens no! A daughter your age? That is not cool. Let me handle this my own way."

They heard Beth chuckling.

"Alright Dad, do it your way, but keep us in constant touch, won't you? I will browse for the schools we need included in the invitation. It's not for the whole of London. And we are targeting, first, South African children. Let's see how many roughly we can expect. If there are too few we can widen our scope to Botswana and Namibia, maybe? And Dad, we will have to lay on the lunch on ourselves. Our treat. "

"Of course darling, naturally," said Richard. "In the end this is your event, and I will abide by your decisions. Text me any thoughts, as I will to you."

"So things are going along excellently," said Oliver, "in the astrosphere. We just have to ground it, but your Dad seems to have all that worked out. He is used to saying 'let it be done' isn't he? I wish I was."

"Oliver! You are just fine as you are. Dad is still psychologically a colonial. He grew up with authority. He's great even now at enthusing people and manufacturing things out of nothing, but his kind are dying out. We have grown up in a different world. We have to work within the system, and your system is the law. You are bound by its rules as I'm bound by the laws of biology and physics. It is painstaking work and we are both in service. We have to obey most of the time. Forget Dad. I like us as we are."

"Oh so do I," Oliver groaned taking her in his arms. "I'm so in love darling....."

Chapter Fourteen

The next morning, back at home, Bridget began to browse schools in Hackney. She decided she would simply ring them up to ask if they had children from a South African back-ground for an event she was organising with a South African ambience. She would tell them what it was if they responded positively. There was a list of twelve Haringey Borough supported secondary schools, of which one was Butler's. Dad was approaching that, so she would ring one of the other eleven if she could figure out the right words.

"Hello! Is that Butler Senior Secondary School please? May I speak to Mrs. Fletcher?......good morning Mrs. Fletcher. My name is Bridget Kendall and I am ringing from Cirencester........yes, a long way away. I am interested in contacting pupils of South African parentage. My father grew up in Cape Town during the time of the apartheid struggle. He met Nelson Mandela, and his parents were activists for the anti-apartheid movement. Besides that he has many happy recollections of his childhood there.........Yes, very interesting. He is retired now and is keen to meet up some young third millennial children whose roots are South African, and share his memories essentially. He is going to hold a cultural lunch during which he will talk about those years, and what it was like to be there. He has Xhosa CDs and a lot of photos, and he will host a South African lunch. The number he can invite is limited so he is inviting the poorer less advantaged of South African children. So we are asking schools in Haringey if they have children of South African origin we can include. The invitations will go to the schools, not to the children personally..........yes, this month, during the last week, after the exams. The actual date will be fixed when we have discussed it with head teachers......you have six? That is great. May I contact you by email setting out the details as far as we have them now. Formal invitations will be sent in the next week or so........thankyou, I've have got that. Can you give me the names of any other schools in your area which have South African children please? Oh they all do. Wonderful. Thank you very much."

She put the receiver down with a sense of accomplishment. So they were inviting children from eight schools. They would need to know rough numbers. She rang her father to give him this latest up-date. He said he would go to the Butler school first to talk with Agnes Fletcher.

He intended in that way to establish his credentials and respectability, he said, and get permission to use her hall!

"A lot depends on this Bridget. If we are going to use her premises to vet children for funding I have to get her permission to do that too. These days an elderly man can't look at a child without the police intervening. I shall tell her my wife and daughter will be with me, and that this is actually my daughter's task. I'm the one who grew up in Africa, that's all."

"It's scary Dad. Grandfather seemed to trust me but I'm not really up to it, and I would be nowhere without you."

"He knew you could handle the actual funding darling, but in fact he had no idea what the modern scene is like in Britain, and how many people are bustling around in the charity business. We hadn't realised that even ourselves. Things are much more complex now than he knew. All this charade is to get to meet up with few actual children in need, face to face."

"Yes. Thanks a ton, Dad. If this works out successfully it will be because of your enterprise."

"I'm keen that it should Bridget, not just to carry out Father's wishes, but for the sake of the children. We are offering, I take it, to pay for tuitions each year to help them get good grades, and be qualified to go to university or take up some other training. We may need to supply laptops. We may need to organise some sort of mentoring to steer them through, and introduce them to the concept of joining a public library. All that will depend on individual home circumstances. The bright bouncy kids you see in advertising photos are where they are because people helped them."

"Oliver keeps talking about wanting to make a difference. Maybe this will give him opportunities he is looking for."

"He's a good man, Oliver. I rather think this is going to present us all with commitment we had not anticipated!"

She began to draft out a letter to school heads notifying them that a South African celebration morning for school children was being organised, and that invitations were soon to be issued. She decided to send the letters by post. So much junk was sent by email and often just went straight to spam. Most of the rest of the initial work was being done by her father, and ordering the lunch would have to be left entirely to him. She hoped he could produce a chatty light-weight talk. Heavy stuff about the back-ground to apartheid would not be appropriate and would probably be boring. Her father wasn't usually boring, but given the chance, he had a lot of steam to let off on that subject. Maybe she should warn him? No. He seemed to know what he was doing. At one o'clock she rang Oliver. He was encouraged to hear how well things seemed to be going. Plans were still in the "astro-sphere" but her father was poised to contact Agnes Fletcher. She read him out her letter to all the school heads, and after a few additions he approved it.

"I'll do the print-outs and post them off this afternoon," she said.

"Good. And we need to think about decorating the hall Bridget. I'll try travel agencies for posters, but in any case I can do print-outs from the internet. Then get a few enlarged. Your Dad's photos will illustrate his talk, but we can add some modern ones. There's no harm in boosting South African tourism while we are on the job."

"Will you handle that Oliver? Dad will order the lunch when we get an idea of numbers. Just now we are waiting to hear how things go with Agnes Fletcher. If we can use her hall the show is on the road."

"Can he speak Xhosa?"

"Oliver! Of course he can. He is bi-lingual. No, tri-lingual. He speaks Afrikaans too. His parents made sure he learnt Xhosa from the beginning."

"Probably the guests don't!"

"I think many will. From what I've seen of immigrant families the natives languages are often used in the home."

"Did he teach you any?"

"Bits. I didn't put any effort into it. 'Molo, unjani?'"

"What?"

"Hello, how are you?"

"I could practise saying that. It will add a bit of local colour. We need videos of Nelson Mandela and other leaders. They can be set up round the room with ear-phones. And posters to show the country, and Cape Town. Yes, I'll work on it."

"Dad will be bringing CDs. I'm beginning to look forward to this!"

Oliver was to come to her house that evening, but she decided to go to Ashcroft Manor that evening, hopefully to meet Sandra. She texted him to say she would leave her key under the gardenia pot near her door.

At half-past five she took her bicycle out of her shed and cycled to Ashcroft Manor. As she did so she thought about her grandfather taking this same route on his bicycle. Was he "breathless" at the thought of being with her, as he described himself as being when he booked a flight to London in two thousand and nine? After passing through the gates of the Manor she took the path to the botanical garden, and leaned her bicycle against the wall. She wandered along the paths on foot, thinking now about Maria. This was her territory, her world. How wonderfully she had created it. The peacefulness was so deep it was almost tangible. Trees of many species grew in abundance and seemed almost to be communicating with her. The plants were labelled carefully, and arranged according to the parts of the world where they grew. There was a greenhouse for some of the more exotic plants. She stood for a while silently communicating back. John and Maria must often have walked here, though at that stage the garden was not nearly so fully developed. Perhaps, she thought fancifully, they walked here again together now?

Just then she heard footsteps approaching and turned to see Sandra approaching.

"Hi," she said, "why didn't you come to the house?"

"Hello Sandra. Yes I was coming to see you really, but thought I would wander here first. I am remembering John and Maria. They must have walked here. Do you think they still do?"

"Definitely, if they can. We should ask my mother. She can always tell."

"This is a lovely garden, Sandra. Do you often wander round it?"

"Yes, it is a favourite spot. There's a seat along here. Let's sit. Of course, you know what life is. One thing after another, and one forgets to take time out. Natasha said she saw you coming in this direction. Was it about anything in particular?"

"Not really. We have started to try and organise a 'celebrate Cape Town' morning in a Hackney School. It was proving too difficult to seek out a few under-privileged children, and Dad came up with the idea of hosting a South African lunch to which children of South African parentage will be invited. There will be lots of paraphernalia to show-case the country, and Cape Town in particular. Dad will host it and talk about his early years there, and generally mingle and chat with the children. Mum and I and Oliver will be there to do the same. The hope is to discover bright children who are not surviving well because of circumstances. Dad will have been talking to a head teacher today, and I have sent out some exploratory letters. I wanted to reconnect with the people who started it all."

"Heavens Bridget, how are you going to get to know any children that well over a lunch? Can't you just ask head-teachers to produce their most deserving pupils?"

"Because it turns out there are loads of schemes already in place to uplift black school-children. There are charities, like at least a dozen. The easy answer is just to donate to existing programmes, but that isn't what Grandfather intended. I want to connect with a few who have fallen through the system, children whose parents for some reason aren't supportive, and whose homes cramp development, so they don't get noticed by the talent-spotters. I don't want to look at children through the eyes of the authorities. I want to find three who have fallen quietly by the wayside, so to speak. We don't have anything like enough money to pay for university or other courses, and why should we? They can get loans like all the other students. Our task, I think, is to get three children up to the finishing-post, that is university entrance level, by providing the support parents would normally be expected to give."

"OK. It sounds good, if nebulous. You mean you will go round chatting to these kids and try to spot some who look neglected."

"Our trump card is Dad. In fact this whole thing is his idea and he is basically organising it, and don't underestimate my Dad."

"I won't, no, and what is he contributing?"

"Well the lunch, for a start, and a talk, and leading the children in general gossip and back-chat, arguing with each other maybe, and being drawn into speaking their minds to each other as well as to us. We want them to take the lid off. We need to unwind them. No teachers present, if we can fix that. I can't do it, Oliver can't, but he can. If we fail, well we'll all have had a good lunch and a party. He can talk about apartheid. He was there, and he was a growing child in the middle of it. Some analogy might be hinted at with those children's own lives. Maybe not. We'll see."

"But your Dad was a white child," pointed out Sandra.

"His parents were anti-apartheid activists, and his mum held secret meetings with women of all colours."

"Right. So he might gain the confidence also of those third millennial children."

"He might. It's all a shot in the dark, and of course it might fail completely. We have to step out in faith Sandra." She grinned. "There must be lots of mantras on that subject. We are doing it literally. We have to be lent a school hall to start with. Dad is working on that as we speak."

"'Faith beyond Fear'? And how is he doing that?"

"He wants to persuade a head teacher, mainly by exerting his charisma it appears. I wasn't to accompany him, as a grown-up daughter isn't cool. He seems to be aiming for groovy or hip, but smart, nothing deceitful. This is very serious, and he will be absolutely frank about what we are doing."

"Well good luck, Bridget. I mean that. I really hope this succeeds. Will you come in for a drink now?"

"Er, no, thanks. Oliver is coming and he must have arrived. But thanks for listening Sandra."

Chapter Fifteen

When she got home Oliver was in her parlour with a mug of coffee, and water was hot in the kettle. He poured out hers and she flopped in the other chair.

"How did your day go Oliver?"

"Oh the usual. I have started collecting photos but I won't bother you with the details."

"I've written to several schools but I won't bore you with that either. Let's relax."

"Yes. I expect your Dad is breezing along."

"I hope so. I doubt that modern Hackney is going to be quite what he expected."

"What was Sandra's reaction?"

"Scepticism. Strangely, for a New Age Reiki healer, whose mother is a professional psychic, she seemed to think it would be simpler and wiser to work within the system. I explained why I felt the system is the thing we specifically want to work outside, and she wished me luck. Funny New Ager she is!"

"Does her mother live round here? I want an appointment."

"Sorry. She's in Wales."

"What does she do as a Reiki healer?"

"She channels the universal energy through her hands into one's body. That re-energises parts of us which have become weak, and re-aligns whatever is askew. I looked it up. They literally put their hands above your body and channel energy. It leaves you feeling invigorated and smoothes away aches and pains."

"If it's possible to do that, which sounds amazing, why don't we get it on the NHS?"

"I *think,* I'm not sure, you possibly can, but not routinely obviously, or we'd know about it. I think it's one of those things which can't be regulated. You can't measure it, so it isn't controllable enough for government purposes. It's spiritual and that alone condemns it as iffy. I don't even know if Maria had any. She seems to have talked to Sandra at least, and in such a way that Sandra considers whatever was said as confidential. But Sandra was a child during Maria's critical years, so we can't know. She does seem to have been interested in the holistic approach to healing and balance, because John compared it with African spirituality. And then mysteriously they developed this powerful spiritual connection or union during which they united in the night in some spiritual realm to transmit spiritual light or energy to the world! How did that come about? They seem to have been turning to spiritual sources of strength, and who can blame them, but there is no explanation of that in the letters. We have to remember they talked on the phone. Wish we had her letters."

"Do you feel temped to give it a try?"

"Not sure. I know Sandra too well now to want to share my soul with her. I have thought of trying it. Are you interested?"

"I just feel all at sea Bridget. You have turned my life upside down, or through you John and Maria have. What spiritual union could they possibly have achieved? John speaks of it as his life-line, his means of surviving separation, which of itself is unusual to the modern mind. How many people now love like that? But it's not just that. It was his way of dealing with his loss. He didn't take anti-depressants. He directed it into something so positive, so powerful, that he became, if he wasn't before, a fighter. Yet he was a solicitor like me. He was trained to measure things by the law, and accept that when judgement is passed that's it. It might be faulty, and it could even be wrong, but it's the best we have to resolve human failure, or downright crime. John rose above that Bridget. The law as laid down by the government was itself criminal in his view, and he was not going to abide by it. He stood up to oppose the law, to break it. How many of our current laws in Britain actually represent justice? How many people who mete out justice actually do just that? And how many realise that they are dealing in fake currency? Am I dealing in fake currency sometimes Bridget? Do the compromises we have to make sometimes to reach a settlement result in the very opposite of justice?" he exclaimed.

"Sometimes they may seem to, but there is a long history behind laws passed in Britain. That means a lot of experience. And Oliver, judges who serve out laughably weak sentences for major crime, maybe because they are taking into account some underlying circumstances, are undermining the law, and you end up with a person charged for a minor offence getting a harsher sentence than another who was responsible for a death. The punishment must meet the crime, and justice has to be seen to be served John. Otherwise you end up with people laughing at the law, and jeering at judges, and mocking the police. Weak justice can never serve the civil society. People aren't spiritual mostly. They will get away with what they can, and if they believe they can get away with a crime lightly, they won't hesitate to flout the law. You get people in some areas afraid to go out at night because the streets are ruled by gangsters the police cannot control, because the courts will just rap their knuckles, and send them back out into the streets with a grudge now against the police who arrested them. You represent order and justice Oliver. You do. And people respect that. Apartheid was an abomination. It might have been the law, but it wasn't justice was it Oliver? It was rank injustice, and that was what Grandfather stood up against. So would you Oliver."

Oliver sat forward with his hands clasped, his face deeply introspective.

"For now I do what I must do. I'm not sure about the long run. You know they talk about a 'calling'. I've got that weird sense of having received one."

Bridget looked at him seriously.

"Have you Oliver? To make changes in the system?"

"Yes. Something like that. It's too vague for me to know yet. What is this universal energy Reiki healers, for instance, somehow manage to link into and channel, and John and Maria seem to have united in?"

"I read that when we sleep our spirits lift out of our bodies into a higher dimension of the spirit, but stay attached to our bodies as long as we live, by a silver cord. That's where the energy is, in the astral dimension, and our spirits absorb energy from the source. Then they return to our bodies rebooted before we wake up refreshed."

"So what does that make the body?"

"Meat, I gather. Our vehicles for this dimension."

"So you are really quite well informed about all this," he smiled at her.

"Don't forget my phone conversations with my grandfather. He talked about balance, and matters of the spirit, from time to time. That was what created the connection between us, which, I imagine, resulted in him trusting me with the ring and the chess-piece, and ultimately the key to his truth. Because he wanted me to carry out a mission for him."

"He wanted to extend a bit of his justice to a few under-privileged kids in London."

"And plant a seed, Oliver, plant a seed. It has been coming over me all day, the wider implications of all this. He could not talk to his son about his most private feelings, (and I would never show Dad his letters), but he knew his son's heart was with him in the essentials. He would have known Dad would support me. He didn't realise I imagine how much I was going to need it, though, because, as Dad himself said, the London of two thousand and seventeen was unknown to him."

"And as a start on the next stage of my journey I am to be involved too," said Oliver wryly.

"Spoken like a true New Age traveller!" she said heartily.

He laughed.

"You are a one-off Bridget. But it runs in the family. I shouldn't be surprised."

"I am feeling capsized too rather. Up till a fortnight ago I was quietly studying soil and plant samples, and my ambition was to work in the arboretum. It still is, but the world has suddenly become so much bigger. Let's have supper. I have made spaghetti bolognaise and fruit salad."

After supper they retired to bed.

"No more talk darling," said Oliver, as they slid into her double bed in the second bedroom. "Just this. Us is what I live for now."

The next morning she received a text from Richard telling her the lunch was fixed for June twenty-seventh in the Josephine Butler School hall, and telling her he would ring when he got home later today. She sent on the text to Oliver in his office. They had to design proper invitation cards and get them printed, but that too would have to be done with Richard. She wondered if he had given any thought to the actual lunch?

"Chicken shisanyama braai," her father told her, "with thick soup consistency pap, and braaibroodjie, which is to say South African garlic bread. Delicious. And for the vegetarians there will be bunny chow, not served as burgers but on a bed of brown rice."

"Right," said Bridget. "What's pap?"

"It's a carbohydrate side-dish made of (in this case) yellow corn starch, water or milk, and butter. The bunny chow is made of mixed vegetables, and there will be salad. The garlic bread will be for everyone as will the pap, and salad. And for dessert, malva. That is a type of chocolate sponge. You can have a big piece or a little piece. "

"What about the first one you mentioned?"

"It is the most delicious marinated barbecued meat with lots of marination made of ginger, black pepper, paprika, fresh garlic, lemon, soya sauce, rosemary, thyme, mixed in sunflower oil. You baste the meat with it. I decided on chicken instead of a red meat, as it would be healthier."

"You know how to cook it?"

"No. I checked with the restaurant about how they make their marination to be sure it would be good. I knew roughly the sorts of things that should go into it."

"Which restaurant?"

"The South African Bistro in Haringey. I have warned them I will be ordering a take-away lunch for the twenty-seventh, and have chosen the menu. I said for at least twenty people, but I would let them know nearer the time. It will be delivered at the school at twelve o'clock."

"Gosh Dad! What about Mrs, Fletcher though? What did she say?"

"Well we had discussion about my limiting the guest list to South Africans, unless there would be too few of them. But since I am the host and am running it, and am going to do the talk about South Africa, she was out-flanked. I suggested this could be a precedent, and next time it could be an Eritrean morning, then a Somali, and so on. At that point she started to get enthused. Children could experience something of their own family cultural backgrounds, and later maybe there will be mixed gatherings. In future families will have to pay contributions of course. Mine is a kick-start."

"Dad, honestly. You've started a whole new movement in order to achieve our actual objectives? Did you tell her about the funding?"

"I couldn't in the end darling. She was a bit limited in her perspective. If I had introduced the idea of funding she would have countered with threats of governing bodies and committees. I would have got nowhere. I will have to approach that from another angle. I'm hoping the local Vicar might turn out to be a kindred spirit. He is the chaplain for the school. Would you like to attend a church service on Sunday at his church with your Mum and me?"

"So now you want the husband and father image. Yes of course, if you think this could be a good approach. I approve of it actually. The Church has pioneered so many things they could not have achieved if they had always been sticklers for protocol. They have a history of barging in. And if you talk to him in confidence he can't betray you either."

"No. Their service is ten on Sunday mornings, and I have to confirm he will be taking the service next Sunday morning. I'll ring him and tell him there is something I would like to discuss. We will be travelling a long way for a church service so I need to know he can see me."

"We need to check trains will be running. It's a long way to drive there and back. I can meet you there."

"It's St. Edwards, Church Lane."

"I will write the formal invitations, then, addressed to head teachers shall I? And we are inviting, for now, children of South African parentage on our list of eight Haringey Borough Council schools? I have already sent an introductory letter to each, outlining the plan, and saying I will confirm the date soon. And I will ask the schools to email me re the number of children who will come. Should we arrange for a bus to go round and pick them up and take them back? Otherwise some will just wander off."

"Good thinking. I will do that. And Oliver is organising modern photos, flags, and apartheid videos I believe? They will play on computers round the room, will they, with head-phones? My approach is historical. It has to be. Of course there is no harm in some modern photographs showing the beauties of South Africa, and its wild-life."

The next Sunday morning Bridget caught an early train for London. She had arranged to meet her parents at the church. It was a sunny day so she wore a yellow dress with a light cream Summer coat, and heels. She hoped to go by tube to Haringey, but if none was running there on a Sunday she would have to get a cab. They decided Oliver should not come, as a fourth new face might seem like an invasion. Church congregations recognised new faces, and were usually curious. She arrived before her parents, and went quietly in to take a seat near the back. It was a Sung Eucharist and she was a confirmed member of the C. of E. So she was perfectly comfortable. The church was Victorian and rather shabby, but the atmosphere was quiet and respectful. Approximately half were white and half black, and there was an Asian family. Her parents slipped in beside her, and the service began.

Of course they were all three scrutinizing the Vicar, and were reassured. He looked like a regular old-time care-worn priest, in his mid-forties. The service proceeded as they expected, with the familiar prayers and readings and hymns they knew. Richard caught the Vicar's eye and registered that he had identified him as the caller. Bridget glanced at her father and realised that he was bracing himself for the conversation. So much depended on his getting support for the funding. She offered up a prayer for the four of them and all those they were inviting. She was sure John and Maria would have rounded up some angels to fight for them. The sermon was on the text, 'blessed are the poor in spirit' which was propitious. Derek Johnson spoke about maintaining a spirit of gratitude which opened the heart to receive the gifts of the Spirit. Good, but she was so on edge, she could hardly concentrate. Hopefully Derek himself would listen to her father with that same spirit of gratitude!

As it turned out she need not have worried. Her parents in their Sunday clothes looked the epitome of middle class Church of England at worship. Her mother wore a green dress with a brown coat and Summer hat, and her father was in dark grey tweeds. They embodied, manifestly, the soul of respectability, and it was on this image of trustworthiness that their case depended. Her mother even wore a pearl necklace, real pearl, with matching ear-rings. At the door as everyone trooped out they exuded charm, and introduced themselves. They were invited to the Vicarage immediately.

"You have come a long way to attend our service," said the Vicar. "It is good to have you."

He didn't seem to have a wife, or at least not present. He offered them coffee, but they refused since presumably he would have to go and make it.

"It is quite a long story Vicar, so I will try to make it short," said Richard. "My father emigrated to South Africa in nineteen-sixty-six, married there, and I was born there. He was a lawyer, but became an activist in the freedom struggle against apartheid. My mother too, who was Africaans, was very much engaged in the resistance, and conducted women's meetings. I grew up in that world, but left when I was eighteen to attend Bristol University. My father died early this year and has entrusted a large sum to my daughter, to direct to three deprived children of South African parentage, who maybe themselves suffered under apartheid. He wanted to help three children attain the necessary standard of education to enable them to enrol in university or any other kind of training. We have discovered that there are any number of schemes already in place to support disadvantaged black children, so we are at a loss how to proceed. We felt we needed to meet three children personally who are in difficulties rather than try to work through organisations. So," he sighed, "I have organised a South Africa morning at the Josephine Butler School. We are inviting children of South African origin in Haringey to come and participate. I shall give an informal talk about my childhood in Cape Town and chat with them, and maybe strike cords in the hearts of any children present who feel they are in some sort of comparable situation in which they do not see any chance of succeeding. We are looking for bright children who would benefit from higher education."

Derek Johnson had listened closely to the story.

"That sounds admirable. Of course there could be technical difficulties, but how can I help?" Richard paused.

"I went to see Mrs Fletcher about the idea, and succeeded in winning her round sufficiently to lend her hall and allow us to make the arrangements ourselves. We sent invitations to seven other secondary schools and await the response. The snag is she wasn't a hundred per cent on board. In her view it is all highly irregular, and I managed to sway her by suggesting that that this could be the first in a series of events celebrating the native countries of local children. In future they would have to be contributory, but this initial event is to be hosted by me and funded by us (though not out of Father's gift money of course). She did think that such an idea was worth thinking about, but she was not enthusiastic enough for me to confide my real objective being to filter out three children to receive funding. Of course we, the three of us and a friend understand that we cannot just hand over large sums of money.

We will have to arrange for tutoring probably, and possibly mentoring, and find space for them to study. Then check on progress. We don't know what it will all entail until we have selected the children. We will make arrangements as we would for our own children, but obviously we have to be trusted. So now I am in a cleft-stick. I can hardly use an event held in Mrs. Fletcher's school to vet children without her permission, and I fear she won't give it. So Vicar, the question is, do you see this plan as having enough merit for you to intervene on our behalf? We need to put it across to her that we are genuine honest people fulfilling my father's request. We will work with the permission of the parents of whoever we select, and only on the basis of their cooperation. Without that we cannot help the child. We will not deal with the children themselves, and we will consult with parents themselves on how best to assist their child. We can call it a scholarship."

Derek Johnson, smiled wryly.

"Yes. I appreciate what it is you wish to do, and I can help you if you will include me in your team. I can't just set you free to intervene in the lives of local families, unsupervised, as it were. My parish will include probably three of your schools, and I can invite the assistance of other clergy. You will need us with you in this if you are not to fall into a host of local traps. And, first and foremost, news shouldn't get abroad that some toffs are handing out money!"

"I would be immensely grateful to have you with us Father," said Richard. "You can vet everything we do. We have no personal agenda. We just want to support three children from around here in exactly the same way we would support our own children."

"Yes, I believe you, but these days everything is regulated. Mrs. Fletcher is quite right to she saw your venture as highly irregular. With child-trafficking and paedophilia at an all time high everything to do with children is closely scrutinised. My own advice would be for you to present this money as a gift to the Church to use for the education of three children. That would cover you. Of course the reputation of the clergy is at an all time low, but we would cover for each other. What is your father's name Mr. Kendall?"

"John Kendall."

"Right, so you could call this the John Kendall Memorial Fund to aid those who have suffered as a result of apartheid. It will provide three scholarships per annum to bright children to complete their secondary school studies, and prepare them for further training or higher studies. The money will be held by you, but will be administered ostensibly jointly with the parish of St. Edwards. The chaplain of the Josephine Butler School will be an authorising signatory to the account. Of course

103

as yet there is money enough only for only the first year, and if further donations don't come in the account will close."

Bridget's face froze, but her father was delighted.

"A man after my own heart! And if we are lucky people will donate and the scholarship will continue! We have time before September and schools re-open to set up the Trust, I suppose it will be."

"Richard," her mother intervened, "this is Bridget's money. Her grandfather asked her to do this. You are racing on ahead without consulting her. I am sorry Father, maybe we didn't make it clear that the holder of the account is my daughter, and the final responsibility is hers. It was a personal request made by her grandfather. "

"Thank you Father, we will think about it," said Bridget. "Supposing I agreed to joint management of the account with the Parish of St. Edward's? Would that mean I would need your signature to make payments, and would it also give you the right to withdraw money yourself?"

Fr. Johnson said,

"It can be a dual signature account, which means I have to counter-sign any payment above a certain amount. It sounds humiliating but it covers you in case of accusations. And the reverse is true that, theoretically, if I wanted, I would not be able to withdraw anything without your signature. Please think it over. I am sorry we were rushing you. It is a device. The name of St. Edwards's Parish on the ticket establishes your credentials in a cynical world. In reality all the books would be in your possession. It no doubt is too ambitious to try to create a Trust. The funding is by its nature for three children only. We will leave it at that. The only change we might make, then, will be that you will need my signature to issue payments. With that in place I can go to Mrs. Fletcher full of joy at your generosity. You have decided to use John Kendall's bequest for the benefit of three of our children in Haringey."

"Fr. Johnson, thank you for being so understanding, said Bridget. "An arrangement like that will suit me perfectly. I have no wish to set up a Trust, or extend my Grandfather's mandate. I accept your suggestion."

Richard watched her, a little disappointed, but respectful. He had promised her that all the final decisions were hers.

"I got a little over-excited Padre," he apologised. "My daughter is far wiser than I. Thank you for listening to me and understanding what we all three really want to achieve in the best possible way. And thank you for promising to intercede with Mrs. Fletcher. The event is to be June twenty-seventh morning at ten. There will be a South African lunch at twelve. We will send you an invitation letter and will be very gratified if you are able to come."

"Thank you Father," said Beth "We are immensely grateful. Are you called Father or Vicar?"

"All sorts. I have been addressed as 'your holiness'. I have a wife but she is away at her mother's with the children this weekend."

"Thank you, Vicar, then," smiled Bridget. "I will talk to my bank about creating a dual signature account."

They exchanged mobile numbers and said goodbye. As they walked away Richard was apologetic for getting too excited and Bridget said,

"It's fine Dad. I wasn't going to jump in out of my depth in any case. You have earned a right to speak your mind."

"I had visions for a moment of a Trust in Father's name, but we have no authority to start asking people for donations. I lost my head."

"Doesn't matter Dad," said Bridget. "Mum and I will always find it for you."

Back, as she felt, safely, in her cottage in Tavistow, she sat in her parlour and rang Oliver. After repeating their conversation with Derek Johnson she said.

"So things seem to be going in the right direction. I am now waiting for a call from him with a report on Agnes Fletcher's reaction. I think coming from someone in a collar she is going to be reassured."

"And Richard has put in a preliminary order for the lunch," said Oliver.

"Yes. He has told them there will be at least twenty. Oliver, can I come over?"

"Of course! You don't have to ask! Come right now."

Chapter Sixteen

Half an hour later she flopped into his brown velvet sofa, looked up at the marble fire-place and gold carriage clock, and sighed with pleasure.

"Don't ever change this, Oliver! It is a refuge from the modern world full of uncertainties, and confusions about right and wrong. This is reality, safe, solid, and we know perfectly well what is good, and what is bad. My grandparents' house was like this, on my mother's side. Granny and Grandpa had a set of old volumes of Punch, and I was allowed to look at them on the dining-table sitting on a cushion on the chair, and turning the pages very carefully, because that was how you treated books. And there were some super special chocolate biscuits Granny kept in the pantry, and as a treat one could have one. The smell from that tin! And being offered one was an occasion. You bit little pieces at a time, and savoured them. Mid-meal snacks of course were not offered, and even the chocolate biscuit was given at the end of lunch. We all knew you didn't eat between meals. Not done." She sighed.

"Now nothing is not done, even placing millions of child pornography photos online for the delectation of thousands of men. How did we get here Oliver? Hold my hand. I'm frightened. Where are we heading?" Oliver was silent for a while.

"At least we know, personally in our own lives, what security is. We know and understand the rules which create safety. We know the things you don't do, and the things you do do. I am stuffy, even in my own eyes, because I was trained to accept those assumptions. And I can't change that. I don't want to. They are my birthright. Those assumptions were what made society, in general, safe. There were always paedophiles but their fields of operation were limited by the law."

"Yes, darling Oliver, the law. Don't ever change."

"I'm thinking that this money opens up an avenue for us, maybe, into a world of fear and uncertainty, where the old rules are no longer time-honoured. Families have been uprooted and trans-planted, and separated from the customs which governed their ancestors, and are no longer enforceable. Just as the Industrial Revolution uprooted our European families and placed them in new environments where the old rules couldn't apply, so, many of those kids do not have the security which the social mores of their elders used to provide, just as did ours."

"And we stride in with the clouds of our ancestral heritages clinging to our ambience to embrace them in a camouflage of security. They, hopefully, will recognise the message, because social mores universally had the same objective of upholding the fabric of society. Our 'good' was their good, and our 'bad' was their bad."

"Yes," said Oliver. "Maybe we can represent a safety they have, in some families, totally lost, as have ours. We just happen to be addressing South African families, though Asian families seem to have, by and large, maintained the rules."

"Which their contemporary generation also seems to be rejecting," pointed out Bridget.

"I question the model of us marching in. I think we will be tip-toeing in, as those going where angels fears to tread," suggested Oliver.

"Yes, it isn't going to be easy is it, and we have already realised before we begin, that largess is not that easy to dispense. Even our fusty Agnes Fletcher is very dubious about a lunch offered for free. There has to be a catch in it. There is of course. She's quite right," said Bridget.

"And the reality is more stunning than the suspicion."

"We do need to think about our demeanour though, don't we?" said Bridget. "That's a constant dilemma for parents. They fear to be authoritative. They try the fellow-kid angle. Doesn't work. Older brother? But you are in fact parents who need to parent. What we are is do-gooders, that hated category of people now, because they assume the right to rule you through their do-gooding."

"So we don't want to look like parents telling them what's what. They will scorn any hint of trying to patronise them. They will jeer at any hint of do-goodery. So who are we?"

Bridget pondered this question for a while.

"I think we might let Dad take the initial step. He's been there. Also the children will know he has. Whatever efforts his parents made, his childhood was not secure Oliver, and as frightening as anything within the experience of London school-children."

"And the children might grant him grudging respect?"

"Well, hopefully. He isn't infallible, and he can run off track. He nearly had me setting up a Trust jointly with the Vicar of St. Edwards, this morning, to be dispensed annually to the needy of East London."

Oliver goggled.

"Yeah. But Dad is manageable. I just told him no. Well Mum said hang on a minute darling first."

"So we ended up NOT setting up a Trust?"

"No. Don't mention it. Dad was embarrassed afterwards."

"So, rehearsing our parts, your father makes initial contact with a likely candidate. You step in as his fairly respectable daughter, under-cover for donor," said Oliver.

"And Mum in the background, easily recognisable as like anybody's Mum, providing the illusion of all being kosher."

"And the Vicar, in collar and not mufti, guaranteeing that this is for real."

"That sort of approach sounds about right don't you think?" asked Bridget.

"I think so. We shall need to prime the cast. Have you had anything to eat?"

"Not since a sandwich lunch."

"OK, I've made chicken fried rice. It seems to be alright."

The next day she had to return to work, and had to ask for June twenty-seventh to be off. She was a bit worried about the on-going liaison work which was bound to follow, so decided to ask for her annual leave. Her manager was not pleased, and she thought it best to explain to him what was going on. Fortunately he was intrigued.

"But that's all very well Bridget. You have on-going work here you can't just abandon."

In the end they decided she would not take her annual leave in a lump, but could take days off when absolutely necessary, and have them deducted from her annual leave. He said he would be able to cover the odd day off. She returned to her laboratory with relief. Nothing like doing the work you loved, and she was deeply interested in the way the landscape changed over the decades and centuries. Like her father she was interested in history, and could integrate what was revealed in the earth with what she knew roughly to be taking place on the surface. Sometimes they found direct evidence of those events in traces of minerals found in the soil. That was always thrilling, and sometimes they had consultations with archaeologists. She had come to realise how her father had moved into a passion for archaeology from his work on the land.

She and Oliver were to travel up to London together early on the twenty-seventh morning in his car. They needed freedom of movement, and did not want to be tied to train-times. Her parents were going up by train. Thankfully the twenty-seventh was sunny. Derek had told Agnes Fletcher the story of the bequest by Bridget's grandfather. A little explanation had convinced her of their authenticity, and even the romance of leaving money for children whose parents had suffered under the apartheid Richard had himself experienced. Derek said the family and a friend would bring photographs and flags, and would set up five videos if she could put five computers in the hall. Richard would bring CDs of South African music and his own player. They would need a couple of trestle tables for the lunch which would arrive at twelve. They would bring cloths themselves, but could she provide school cutlery? It turned out there would be twenty-five children of ages ranging from twelve to seventeen. A bus, he said, was to be hired to pick them up from their schools and take them back.

Bridget and Oliver set off in a mixture of happy expectation and sheer fright. Her father expected hitches, but was unfazed at the thought.

They were impressed by the building. It was modern with lots of glass. Inside everything was clean and as sweet-smelling as a school full of children can be. The woodwork was polished and all the windows and floors clean. They were greeted by a smiling touched-up-blond lady of about fifty. She was not at all fusty and seemed very pleased to meet them. She took them through to the hall which was large.

"Derek has had to excuse himself today," she said, "as there is a diocesan meeting, but of course he told me you have ulterior motives in this. While not mentioning money he and I have asked head-teachers to identify to me any of their children who they think are deprived or under-privileged. That will make things much easier in the short time we have available."

She gave Bridget a piece of paper listing six children under the names of their schools.

"Of course you must judge for yourselves and you can interview any of them here later, but these are the ones the other schools have drawn my attention to."

"Thankyou so much Mrs. Fletcher," said Bridget. "This will be an enormous help.

"The children will wear ID cards to help them talk to us and each other. I gather that apart from the talk you would like an informal atmosphere in which they can talk to you and each other in a free and easy manner. I shall need to be present, but no other staff will be in the room."

Meanwhile one of the maintenance men was talking to Richard and Oliver about the placement of the photos and posters. The hall was large, and thirty chairs had been arranged three rows at one end in front of the table and chair placed for Richard. Two trestle tables stood down one side, and at the back there were schoolroom tables and chairs. Several notice-boards hung on the walls for photographs, and soon they were all busy decorating the room. They had brought two big flags which they erected at the front along with two pots of tropical plants Bridget had borrowed from Ashcroft. They all agreed as they looked round when the job was done that everything looked splendid. Beth had brought African-print table-cloths she didn't mind food getting split on for the tables. The room was looked bright and welcoming. Agnes showed her other teachers round the room to give them a flavour of something they could imitate later.

The bus arrived at ten and twenty-five children trooped in. The younger ones were led to the front row, but otherwise they sat where they wanted. A lot of them already knew each other and there was a lot of waving and greeting. The grown-ups took chairs at the back.

Agnes went to the front first. She clapped her hands to quieten the children, and introduced Richard. She drew their attention also to Bridget and her mother. Then she spoke a few introductory words about the South Africa of their parents' time, and said probably many would have heard about those days. She told them that Richard Kendall had himself grown up in Cape Town, and that though he was white his parents had both been part of the anti-apartheid resistance movement. In spite of all the negative experiences of those difficult times, he had fond memories of his childhood there, and wanted to spend time with children from the same background as his own. Richard then stepped forward and said,

"Wamkelekile! Molweni! Ninjani?"

There were whoops and cheers from the audience and someone called out,

"Ndiphilile enkosi, unjani wena?"

To which Richard replied,

"Ndiyavuya ukukwazi. However I shall speak in English now. Anyone wanting in-depth discussion in Khosa may come to me at the end. As Mrs Fletcher told you I am Richard Kendall. My father was English and went to Cape Town in nineteen-sixty-six to work for a law firm there. He married an Africaans lady and I was born in nineteen-sixty-six. It took him a while to understand what was going on in the country. On the face of it Cape Town was one of the most spectacularly beautiful cities in the world built along the shore of the Cape, with the famous Table Mountain looming over it from behind. I hope you have been there, or if not will go there. You can take a cable car ride to the top of the Mountain to see the most magnificent views, and possibly visit the Nature Reserve up there. The city is modern, and the buildings tall and beautiful. There are parks and monuments, lots of trees, fountains, and of course the sea lapping up on its' shore all the time, and there is a harbour full of ships and yachts.

But there was a very dark side to life in South Africa when my father moved to work there. In the centre of Cape Town near the harbour and the town centre there used to be an area called District Six. It probably is still called that. The population there was cosmopolitan and of mixed race. Residents later described their community as being one big happy family, but in 1966 it was suddenly declared a whites-only zone, they thought because it was prime land in an advantageous location.

Seventy thousand blacks and coloured people were evicted from their houses, and their homes were bulldozed to the ground. The people were taken out of the city and put individually in different places. Now they were to live in blacks-only, or coloureds-only areas away from the town. Many families were split up because of mixed marriages. The apartheid authorities claimed that inter-racial communities bred violence and crime. The Dutch Reformed Church was the main church, and it taught that it was God's will that the white majority, which they said, was more advanced should be preserved and not swallowed up by less developed races.

It took quiet sustained courage on the part of a great many people to fight apartheid, but many whites also engaged in the struggle, particularly the women. My mother was Afrikaans but she was one. They said apartheid was not compatible with Christianity. Apartheid leaders claimed the non-whites preferred to be separate. They said it was a practicality to separate the communities. The blacks were placed in shanty towns. They were issued with passes to authorise them to go anywhere else. They called these the "dumb passes". They had to show to them go to into town to their places of work. Many people were arrested because of some ID pass misdemeanour. An Act had also been passed called the Immorality Act which stated that sexual relations between people of different colour was illegal. The Department of Offences policed what people did, and followed them round, spying on them, to make sure they did not have sexual relations with someone of a different colour. People were arrested for meeting someone of a different colour. Plays were written and performed to show the horrors of apartheid.

There was a prison on Robin island, and Nelson Mandela, who was an anti-apartheid activist and leader, was put there in 1964. Everywhere the blacks were separated from the whites. There were even separate entrances to buildings. Separate transport. The black people had no vote. The Africa National Congress was formed in 1912 but wasn't legalised until 1990. They started their campaign with violence in 1960. Nelson Mandela took over the leadership and was arrested as a terrorist. Prison conditions were very harsh and their occupation was breaking rocks, but they were all incarcerated together and they talked and discussed together the future of Africa. Nelson Mandela managed to get messages carried out of the prison for him to activists outside. Whites were told he was a terrorist.

111

I grew up in the middle of all this turmoil. Often schools were closed because of the riots. I, however was very lucky in that both my parents were active in the anti-apartheid movement. My mother held, or was part of, many clandestine women's meetings to discuss strategies to use against the government. Such activities were classified as treason and those women of all colours risked their lives in the effort. My father took up many cases of people arrested for ID pass infringement, or immorality. He defended black clients in court for free, and he too risked his professional status and his life. I however was protected. Often I had to be educated at home because of the violence, and my parents protected me from seeing atrocities, and by atrocities I mean like a pregnant girl of sixteen crossing a road innocently, and a police-man coming up to her an shooting her for no reason whatsoever. Random shootings by the police were common. My parents would take me out of the city, when they could, to show me the beauties of the country and of Nature, They fostered in me a love of wildlife, and a concern for the environment. They were so successful that I came to England in 1984 to join Bristol University to do a degree in ecology.

In 1976 the government issued an edict saying that the medium of instruction in schools would be Afrikaans. There was an immediate huge protest. My mother immediately opposed it, even though it was her mother tongue, and meetings were held in our house on methods of boycotting Afrikaans. In Soweto, north of Cape Town, thousands of school children took to the streets to march in protest, and the police shot at them brutally. Hundreds were killed and many others seriously injured. They said twenty thousand school children had taken to the streets that day. Most people wanted English and their indigenous language as the medium of instruction. Bishop Tutu, who was bishop of Lesotho at that time, called Afrikaans the language of the oppressor. A Dr. Edelstein who worked for the social welfare of the black population was stoned to death during the Soweto uprising. All the windows were broken and the glass fell into the streets. People remembered afterwards walking on broken glass.

The ANC adopted a policy of making the country ungovernable. To this end rioting broke out and schools were burnt. Afrikaans themselves started to protest and stand up against apartheid. Then, no newspapers could be published in black townships in order to create blackout of black news. Anti-apartheid movements started all round the world. In 1989 De Klerk replaced P. W. Botha as President, and he decided to end apartheid. He launched a referendum, and South Africa voted against apartheid. The people of Cape Town, led by the Mayor and Bishop Tutu, marched in support of peace, and an end of apartheid.

De Klerk released Nelson Mandela in nineteen-ninety-one, and negotiated with him to replace apartheid with universal suffrage. Mandela said, "we have to make this work". He became President in nineteen-ninety-four. Desmond Tutu was Archbishop of Cape Town until nineteen-ninety-six. There was euphoria amongst blacks, but the whites were terrified, so Mandela wanted reconciliation. The Truth and Reconciliation Commission was established in nineteen-ninety-six, and Afrikaans and other whites could come forward and confess what they did, and beg for amnesty.

This brought in a whole new era of democracy. Former residents of District Six who were still alive were invited to move back and rebuilding started.

This morning I would like us to reflect on these events which are part of the history of most of us here. Was the spirit of apartheid limited to that period of history in South Africa, or do we still encounter the same attitudes today? Can you think of places, or instances, where those old attitude of colour discrimination or race discrimination still prevail without the law doing anything to stop them? Are there patterns in our society which echo even now the spirit of apartheid? Can you think of instances in even your own lives which seemed like apartheid? What are the ways we can in our time stand up against racial bias? The issue is far from dead. Please feel free to ask me questions or address each other as long as we can all hear. Richard leaned against the table to signal that the ball was no in the children's court.

One boy put up his hand,

"Sir, did you ever watch the Springboks?"

Everybody laughed.

"I did indeed. Our team could not join in the World Cups of 1987 and 1991 because of anti-apartheid boycotts, but we won all three tests in Australia in 1971, and in 1976 they beat the All Blacks 3-1. I was taken to see them whenever it was possible, but I left the country in 1984.

"Sir, did you ever get into fights?"

"Yes, I did, and came home bloodied a few times, but my parents weren't pleased. They said my vocabulary should be good enough for argument. They did not want me resorting to fists, unless of course it was necessary!"

The children laughed.

"I got into a fight at our school because someone insulted me," said another child.

"So did I," said several others.

The show was on the road. There were serious questions about what happened to people who rioted or marched, how many believed the teaching of the Dutch Reformed Church on black people, what the houses were like to which the people from District Six were relocated, the attitude of the Afrikaans to Nelson Mandela, what Desmond Tutu taught in his churches about apartheid, how far was De Klerk really anti-apartheid, or had he had to just give in, what sort of school Richard went to, and other questions about South Africa generally, such as the sports facilities and what was available for black children. Then some children started talking about insults they had received personally in school, favouritism, as they saw it, to white children, the difficulty of comprehending advanced English text in their school-books when Khosa or some other African language was the language spoken in the home. The children started to argue and discuss among themselves, and Richard had to remind himself that they needed to move on to the social part of the event when music would be put on and the children could watch the videos and inspect the photographs.

He clapped his hands and told them he was now going to play South African CDs, and they were invited to look round. Anyone wishing to talk to him was welcome to do so. He then turned on the first of his CDs. He asked them if they could vosho, which was a South African dance. He said he was too old to demonstrate it, but if anyone could do it, please do. Some came forward and started to do it to the music he had put on. Immediately they were all having a go, and Richard had to re-direct them to the videos.

He had brought a video showing the Soweto uprising, one about whites only, and one showing students walking into Parliament in session. Then there was a you-tube video of clips from Nelson Mandela's speeches and interviews. How vibrant they still were! One began, "I have fought very firmly against white domination", another, "I have refused to be drawn into the differences between various communities that exist in the USA", and, "why are you so keen that I should involve myself in the internal affairs of Cuba and Lybia?" This video was placed at the back of the room so that it could be listened to without ear-phones. Another video showed clips from Mandela's speeches to the United Nations. The children were eager to see excerpts from what was their own history which made them proud, and were inspired to browse more on you-tube when they got home.

Bridget had identified a seventeen year old boy on her list called Sikelela Unako. She smiled at him and invited him to come and meet her father. She asked him if he spoke Khosa. When he said he did, she asked him to try it out on her Dad.

"This is Sikelela, Dad," she said, introducing the boy.

"They call me Cycle," put in Sikelela. Bridget smiled,

"Do you mind?"

"No, it's OK," he said. "They talk to you when they can say your name."

"Well it's usually wise to be pragmatic," said Richard. "Tell me what you are doing."

He glanced at Bridget, knowing this must be one of the kids with issues. She left him to it. The next minute she realised they were talking in Khosa, and Sikelela was standing close to him and talking quietly. Oh good. Never mind the money. A lot of these children might be grateful for a willing ear. Uprooted and trans-planted to a foreign land, even if they were actually born here. She could see her father was taking him seriously.

Another child on her list was Glory aged fourteen. She took Glory to her mother.

She decided to take Iyana Nkosi and Zola Maseko, two girls, herself. Two boys, Mandla Luthando, and Nomlanga Nangamso, she kept for Oliver. She identified Mandla and introduced him to Oliver, and then took Iyana to one side to ask her what she was doing. This was merely an introductory remark, and she went on to comment n what a pretty name Iyana was. She was a sweet-faced mature girl of sixteen. She commented intelligently on what she had heard about apartheid. She also remarked on how strong the sense of community the black and coloured South Africans seemed to have had. It was so good to hear about the women of all races coming together for joint action in Richard's house, and in others, she expected. Bridget said,

"Yes, I am told they had meetings regularly but clandestinely in each of their houses at no fixed time or date. They arranged it verbally at each meeting. They were risking their lives, and those of their families.

"To do that though," said Iyana, "you had somehow to get together people of one mind, and that in itself must have been difficult."

"You are right," said Bridget. "It must have been. Relating those past events to the present day, if she were able to bring together a group of women in the same way, what changes would she like to make in society?" Iyana was interested, and thought for a moment.

"I think a feeling of community, at least among that group. So many women need help. Child care is a constant problem, lifts for those who need them to get to hospital, advice, they would be like a brigade, all for one and one for all, and put their names on whatsapp under a name called something brigade, or fellowship. Then whoever needed help could post it on whatsapp, and the others would be bound to do something, as if they were all sisters." Iyana's face was animated with her vision. Bridget was interested.

115

"That sounds totally brilliant," she said sincerely. "Maybe one day you can form one. Do you have any real sisters?"

"Yes, but she's only five. She has a twin brother, so they are a handful."

"Yes," agreed Bridget, "especially getting them off to school in the morning."

"Yes," sighed Iyana, "their lunch boxes, their PE kit, putting on their shoes, making sure they cleaned their teeth."

"You sound as if you do it," commented Bridget.

"I do. Mum is disabled."

"Oh my God," exclaimed Bridget, "so you mean you have to get the twins washed and dressed, and give them their breakfasts, and take them to school?"

"A friend of Mum's takes them but they have to wait for me to collect them."

"What happened to your Mum?"

"She and Dad had a car crash. He was killed."

"Iyana, I'm so sorry!" exclaimed Bridget. "Don't social services help out?"

"They come in three times a day to look after Mum, but they feel that with a daughter of sixteen we can manage the little ones. We can of course."

"What do you want to do when you leave school?"

"Go to University, but I don't think that will be possible. I don't get time to study. The children need their supper, and to be put to bed, and then they won't go to sleep. Mum can't walk. Her spine was fractured."

Tears came into Iyana's eyes, and she wiped them away.

"Sorry," she said.

"No, no, in your place I would cry."

Iyana caught the eye of a friend and excused herself.

Bridget moved on round, looking for Zola. She knew the child to be fifteen, so scanned the middle-height range girls and spotted her. She had quite long shiny hair tied up in a pony-tail, and she was pretty and petite. There was a sparkle in her eyes. Bridget approached the girl with a smile.

"Zola? Hi. Did you like my Dad's talk?"

"It was good. He is funny. Can he really vosho?"

"I expect so. He spent his teenage years in Cape Town."

"It wasn't much fun though back then," said Zola.

"True, but young people have a knack of making their own fun. What do you do in your spare time Zola?"

She had some difficulty with that question. Finally she said,

"I'm trying to learn to play the piano. That's what is fun for me, and I am trying to make it. I want to study music, but my father says unless you are brilliant at it, it isn't a career. So I sneak to a friend's house and he is teaching me for free."

"That's amazing. How old is he Zola?" said Bridget anxiously, grimacing inwardly at herself for this maiden auntish concern, but you "never knew".

"He's twenty, so he is quite old. He wants to form a group. He plays the piano and guitar himself, and he's got a friend who's practising drums. I am going to join his group on the piano if I can get good enough. We don't have a piano though so I have to practise at his house."

"Don't your parents know about the lessons then?"

"No, but it's alright. His sister is part of the group. She doesn't want to learn an instrument, so she plays the triangle! She is very funny. And his Mum is there. She gives us snacks. His parents are fine with the group idea."

"Does your friend have a job?"

"Yes, he's an electrician."

"So he is training the group in his spare time. His parents won't mind that."

"For me it is different though. I want to go to University. Dad says good, but not to do music."

"Zola the idea is great, but you do need to tell your parents. You are learning in your spare time so why would they mind that? Presumably you do your school homework?"

"Yes, but my grades aren't too good. What's the point if I have to do some boring job at the end of it all? I can get a job as a hair-dresser or something."

"Zola, what you are telling me is very interesting, and I'ld like to help, but your first job is to talk to your parents. I can get you a piano, but the whole plan must be out in the open first." Zola gaped at her.

"Really! But why?"

"My grandfather loved South Africa and he was always keen to help young South Africans here if they showed promise. Of course I have no idea if you do, but learning to play the piano is a big plus in anybody's life. It's no great tragedy if you don't get to be a concert pianist."

Zola's face drooped.

"That's what I really want to be though, in the end. Playing in a group would be the start."

"Right," said Bridget, "OK. Let's stick to the present for now. I will get you a piano if you talk to your parents, and get their permission to learn. The next absolute condition is you work at your school lessons to get good A levels, and promise your parents you will. What does your father do? Does your mother work?"

"Mum is a carer. Dad is a truck driver."

"Can they afford piano lessons?"

"I guess so," she said.

"Well listen Zola, we will keep in touch. I'll give you my whatsapp number. Let me know when you have got permission from your parents to have a piano, and we will take it from there. I can help only if you put in the hard work. Why not get them to meet your friends' parents? They sound nice people, and if your parents like them they will probably allow you to make music with their children. See, this is my card you can show them. I am an environmental scientist in Cirencester. Your parents can ring me or email me any time. Oh! Here's our lunch. Bye for now Zola."

Zola stared after her dazed, and looked down at the card in her hand.

Bridget made straight for Oliver and grabbed his arm. He turned and looked down at her with a smile, and her heart melted. He was her refuge now, somehow, whenever she was nervous or disturbed. That conversation had taken it out of her! She was used to plant-training. Making life-altering offers to a sensitive girl of fifteen, who was also a complete stranger, had pushed her boundaries. Whew!

Anyway the lunch looked and smelt promising! It was being borne into the room in very large stainless steel serving-bowls by four men from the restaurant. They arranged the bowls expertly on the tables, and put their own serving spoons alongside them. The children watched in anticipation. They were all deeply intrigued, and as the lids were removed Richard introduced the menu to everyone as if the dishes were newly arrived guests. To him they were, and he hoped the children would enjoy them. To many of the children they were a familiar sight, and "wow"s could be heard round the room. School plates had been piled up on both tables along with spoons and forks, so the children were invited to help themselves. The over-fourteens were expected to stand round the room to eat, but classroom tables and chairs had been placed at one end of the room for the younger children.

The meal was noisy and the children laughing and excited. Bridget and Oliver and her parents moved round in amongst them, asking about where their parents came from and what they were doing in London. It was an enlightening experience for the three of them whose lives had been sheltered but Richard was in his element speaking bilingually and making jokes in both languages. All the children wanted to say something to him and get his attention and smile. Bridget was fascinated to witness her father off the leash, and letting it all out. Music was put on quite loud and after the plates were removed the children started to engage in impromptu dancing. The adults joined in, and the rest of the school wondered what the hullaballoo could be. Those who could see wished they could join the party. Finally it all wound down and Agnes announced the bus had arrived to take them all back to their schools. This was followed by groans. Many of the children had exchanged phone numbers. They remembered, as they had been instructed, to thank Richard and Agnes Fletcher, and then trooped out to the bus.

The grown-ups collapsed on chairs to recover.

"Well that went well," remarked Oliver.

"It was wonderful!" exclaimed Agnes. "I can't thank you enough really. It all seemed so extraordinary I was freaked out, as they say. You get reprimanded for much less than holding a function for one particular race these days, with unvetted guests, but Derek vouched for you so I took the risk, and it was a ball! Fantastic morning. I shall definitely do this again with other groups, though in future they will have to be in the name of integration. That was the word lacking in this morning's gathering, and I shall have to fluff it a bit with the authorities, but those children were so happy! And you all seemed to be offering one-on-one counselling where needed. They wouldn't have opened up to us, but your Khosi Mr. Kendall, and your personality went straight to their hearts. Thank you, all of you."

"Thank *you*, Mrs. Fletcher," responded Richard. "We have everything to thank you for in allowing us to come. I don't know how we would have got our job started without local help, and you provided it. Our first predicament was how to make contact less privileged South African children at *all!*"

"Well please keep me informed about how it all goes," she said.

It was time to excuse themselves, so they checked that the men from the restaurant had cleaned up after themselves, collected their photographs, and departed.

Chapter Seventeen

They had agreed to meet at a Starbucks afterwards to discuss findings, since Richard and Beth would be returning to Chedworth. Oliver had found the nearest outlet and drove them all there. Fortunately it was not very full so they could select a table to themselves. Oliver took their orders and for a few minutes they just sat unwinding.

"I really enjoyed myself," remarked Beth. "Glory's problem is more attitude, I thought, Bridget. She has a bit of a chip on her shoulder in general and is fed up with her mum in particular. I just spent time listening to her angle on things and tried to explain that like to a large extent is what you make it. Childhood is soon over, and the best preparation for life, long-term, is to get good grades so you have freedom to make the life-choices you want. I did feel her mother wasn't the best, but I suggested she keep her eye on her own ball instead of wasting time trying to change things. In the short time available I thought the best thing was to boost her self-image and a can-do frame of mind. I didn't see funding as a solution in her case."

"Brilliant Mum, "said Bridget. "I also felt that the event was a lot more than about money in the end. Every child needs to be heard, and I thought we all put in our best on that. We did our best to listen to their stories, and bolster their morale. Adolescence is no picnic. How about you Dad. What did you make of Sikelela, or Cycle?" Her father looked serious.

"That kid has a serious problem which we will have to think about. Let's leave mine till the end. How did you get on with your boys Oliver?"

"Good kids basically, both of them. I jotted notes on my phone. Mandla Luthando. He is one of a big family where the father drinks, and can't hold down a job. His mother holds things together on her nurse's salary, but she doesn't have time or energy to watch what her children are getting up to, and the father is blotto. So the two older boys are now in gangs and drug dealing. It's very lucrative. Mandla hasn't got there yet, so, like you Beth, I concentrated on the subject of life-choices and the future long-term. He can make his life or break it. I asked him if he would like me to grass his brothers to the police, and he said yes! He's not safe and he's scared to death. I've got their names and the address, so will intervene on that one. I'll come up to London to see what I can do. It will take time, but again this is not about funding. I told him I am his solicitor, or lawyer, now and if ever there is any trouble I will represent him. He has my whatsapp number, but I said if he lost it I can always be reached through Mrs. Fletcher."

"Be careful Oliver," warned Richard. "Gangland is a lawless world."

"But the law is my protection and defence here, Richard. If it isn't, what's the point of it?"

"Anyone can drift beyond the law, Oliver, with the best possible intentions. And the law won't protect you out there. It's tooth and claw." Bridget looked at her father, startled.

"You mean Oliver could find himself in a mess."

"Anyone can, with the best possible intentions naturally, because the law doesn't cater for anomalies and irregularities. Everything that goes on just doesn't fit the shape."

Bridget glanced at Oliver, and saw him looking at Richard closely.

"I'll be careful, Richard," he promised. "Then Nomlanga Nangamso. Again, nice guy. great guy. He's supposed to be going to university, in fact, but he has told his parents he won't go. He's one who wants to change the shape. Don't we all? He isn't a conformist, and sees it all as the rat-race that ends you up with a 2x2 family and a bungalow. Not for him! No siree. He's got other plans he won't divulge. His family has been complaining to the school that they have been indoctrinating him with left-wing bs to the extent that now he wants to go out there and save the world. Of course I tried to put to him the bit about the advantages of having a degree under your belt as you set off, but I ended up agreeing with him on the whole. I've been there. He doesn't require intervention. I just wished him well, gave him my card in case he ever needs a free lawyer, and left him to it. I shall watch his future with interest."

"Gosh, Oliver, you had a tough morning," said Bridget. "So did I. My first possible needs help, but I'm not sure what form it should take. She is Iyana Nkosi, aged sixteen. Her parents had a car accident which killed her father and left her mother disabled. She can't walk. Social services come in three times a day to care for her, but leave five year old twins, pretty much for Iyana to look after, figuring she's old enough and quite capable. But two five year olds are a handful, and she nearly wept over saying, 'they won't go to sleep'. She is very keen indeed to go to university but sees no hope of putting in the study. She spoke eloquently about her idea of women (with reference to Louise, Dad) forming groups, or brigades, she called them, putting their names on of course, whatsapp, and being available to each other a hundred per cent whenever anyone needed help all for one and one for all, she said. I don't know if social services will step in to help her as a minor carer? Otherwise we employ a nanny house-helper for the next five years so Iyana can do her thing. We have to mull that over.

Then there's this bright spark, Zola Maseko. She wants, ultimately, to be a concert pianist. The first snag is they don't have a piano, and the second is her father says there's no future in music. She wants to do a degree in music, but no way Jose. She is allowed to go to university to study something sensible. So, she's made friends with some guy aged twenty, who plays the guitar and the piano, and wants to form a group. He's got a drummer, and his sister plays the triangle, and he has promised Zola she can join if she gets to play the piano well enough. To that end he is giving her lessons on his own piano. The family sounds to be decent, but Zola, as she puts it, sneaks, there for lessons. I have promised her a piano, chaps, I hope that meets your approval, on the condition that she tells her parents about the lessons, and introduces them to the family. The other condition is that no matter what she ends up doing, she will work hard at her studies and get good grades, and she will promise her parents to do so. She can whatsapp me when she's talked to her family and got permission for the kind gift of a piano from an environmental scientist in Cirencester. I told her if she works hard I will help her swing the music degree plan, if she does indeed show talent. A lot of discussion will have to go into that, and we will all consult on it. Dad, what about Sikelela Unaki?"

Richard clicked on to details he had jotted in his mobile.

"He's illegal," he said looking round at them all. "So we have what they call 'a situation'. The Unaki family are from Cape Town. Sikelela is an only child and his mother ran off with another man. His father, Themba, had this brother in London called Uuka. He is settled here and working for Transport for London, and is married to Akhona. They have two daughters called Buhle and Esihle. Themba worked as a builder in Cape Town. When his wife ran off he was left to bring up the boy by himself. As a result he decided to come to his brother in London. He had no qualifications, and if he had got a tourist visa he would be in the records. So he thought it would be better to slip under the radar and enter via Shannon airport. That is what you do apparently. All you need is your ticket and evidence of somewhere to stay on arrival, which is a hotel reservation. You then go to Belfast or Dublin, and take a ferry to the mainland. No questions asked. Thus there were no records of his presence in London. Uuka took him in, and managed to get him a job as a builder. They could get permission for Sikelela to attend his cousins' comprehensive school as a visitor. The girl cousins call him their brother anyway, and Themba had shown considerable initiative in procuring a fake birth certificate for him in Cape Town announcing Sikelela's father was Uuka! Nice."

His eyes flicked to Bridget.

"Sikelela turned sixteen in two thousand and sixteen. Then his father was apprehended on a building-site where he was working, and later deported. He just said nothing about having a son, so Sikelela is still here, ostensibly Uuka's son. Uuka and Akhona kept quiet, and he continues to go to school with his cousins. He is very bright and doing well, and wants to be a mechanical engineer. He thinks he can get the grades for university, but he is also an illegal."

Richard leaned back and sighed.

"Cycle, (they call him Cycle), told you all this!" exclaimed Bridget.

"Yes, speaking Khosi like a native does wonders sometimes. He believes I will help. I'd love to! Do I follow Uuka and Akhona's example and just say nothing too, Oliver?"

"Oh definitely for now."

"And we can just go home and keep quiet. I do agree, but the question is his future. If he is to seek higher education he's going to need more than a fake birth certificate. Uuka has managed very well for him. He's registered at the local surgery as Uuka's son, Mother disappeared, which is true. What do you think Oliver?"

"I think I definitely need to go back to the drawing-board and go into family law. Richard, would you like to leave this to me to enquire into discreetly? I shan't betray Cycle of course, but there should be ways round this."

"Like illegal ways?" suggested Richard quizzically.

"Well, yeah, I mean if push comes to shove. Are we all agreed that no matter what course of action we decide to take, we will not grass up Cycle?"

"Agreed," they all said.

"The simplest solution is some more fake something-or-others," said Richard.

"Except we don't know where you get them, good ones," said Bridget.

"It's an industry," said Oliver. "I expect I can find out, but before that I will try my best to find a decent legal solution which will provide him with proper papers."

"Thank you Oliver," said Beth. "We'll do what we have to in the end, but the legal way is infinitely the best! We just can't destroy his life if that proves impossible, that's all."

"Meeting adjourned," said Richard. "We have to go. Come to our house for confidential meetings," he said to Oliver and Bridget. "Otherwise we'll phone or text."

On the way home in the car Bridget asked,

"Oliver, would you describe yourself as left-wing?"

"No. If I have a hero he is Winston Churchill. The left aren't good for law. They don't see it as a thing, standing like a pillar in its own right, a thing against which other things are to be measured and judged. They see it as a set of rules to be bent and adjusted to suit the circumstances of the offender. It is relative. If a guy had a bad home, the law says oh well we mustn't judge him too harshly. And if he killed someone it's hard lines for the victim's family but if they are more privileged or there are other attenuating circumstances which give the victims an advantage over the killer, a lighter sentence will help balance the wrongs suffered by the criminal. An alternative subjective interpretation of justice in his particular case is therefore put in place, because they claim, it wasn't essentially his fault. That view of law makes a mockery of the entire justice system. It undermines the authority of the police, and indeed of the courts and the judges. No I am not left-wing."

"But you are prepared to bend the law for Sikelela," said Bridget.

"Break it, Bridget, not bend it. The law is still the law. If I break it I shall be culpable. *I* will break it, incidentally, not you, if anyone ends up getting arrested."

"My hero, but let's hope it doesn't come anywhere near that. We are going to handle this very carefully, Oliver."

"We will. Are we going to my house?"

"Oh yes, let's," she said.

Chapter Eighteen

That evening after meal of chicken salad which Oliver had left prepared that morning, they relaxed in his sumptuous, as Bridget thought it, drawing-room.

"So, what do we think?" she asked. "I will write up written reports on mine, as I think they both qualify for help, Iyana very much so, Zola, yes but how is yet to be considered. I have told her I will get her a piano if she is frank with her parents, and applies herself to her school-work. We can arrange for training if she shows promise as a pianist and needs more professional teaching than probably her parents can provide.

For Iyana I would like to find a live-in nanny-cum-household help for five years, if the local authorities can't help. I shall start on that straight away on that by finding out about what social services in fact could do if we push.

Sikelela is a third must. You have extended help and support to Mandla, which is brilliant, so he is very much on our list as someone possibly needing funding in the future, but we don't know. So we have probably definitely, Sikelela, Iyana, and Zola. Do you think that is right?"

"Yes, but we need to be very flexible. We don't know how any of the situations might develop. Can we take it that John won't mind if we think things out as we go along, and possibly modify or change course if any of the children doesn't follow-through as we expected?"

"He just gave me the money. That left me free, and I think we have to use our common sense. We are four to contribute opinions, and agree on final decisions. Of the four one is his son, and one his grand-daughter. I think we have to play it by ear a lot of the time."

"Agreed. Incidentally when it came to the crunch I had no problem whatsoever in abandoning my stuffy side in favour of my pragmatic side. Did you notice?"

"I certainly did Oliver. John thought nothing either, apparently, of getting a fake birth-certificate for Richard n order to protect Maria. He is our role model in this since he gave us the money. You are doing him proud!"

Oliver laughed.

"It was an eye-opener of day wasn't it? I feel knackered. Your father was in his element though wasn't he, a born host."

"Yeah, any party goes if he is there."

"In that short time we shared, in imagination, the very different life-stories of six kids, all completely different and all absolutely compelling. It was a pity we couldn't hear about all their lives, though I think we did the best we could in the time available. The names forwarded to us from the schools turned out to be crucial in pointing us in the right direction. In each case there was an issue, if not all needing intervention."

Her mobile rang. It was Richard.

"Hello Bridget? Things seemed to go well didn't they?"

"They really did Dad, thanks to you. Your idea, your organisation, and the fantastic lunch, the music, and even vosho! It was your party and it was magnificent. Even our most difficult challenge was found in the child you talked to. Grandfather should just have asked you to handle this. Did he think it would be educational for me? If he did, he was right. Even Oliver feels sand-bagged."

"Sand-bagged? Shouldn't that be 'wind-bagged'? No, no. I think they say 'wiped out'. It was stimulating though wasn't it? And out of such a small group of kids you uncover so many serious issues. It has healed me, though, Bridget."

"What? How Dad?"

"All that stuff about my fake birth-certificate? 'How dare he?' 'What an insult to Mum!' 'And he a lawyer!' Well I know now. Sikelela's father did the exact same thing for *his* son, even sacrificing his right to be named, to give the boy a better future, and save him, hopefully, from deportation. My Dad ensured my security, potentially, in South Africa because my mother was a South African national, and he protected Maria. People do these things for those they love. I shouldn't have been foaming at the mouth. He had his priorities right. "

"Yes, I think so, Dad. He was in a quandary wasn't he? Anyway, glad you feel more comfortable with it. Did Mum enjoy it?"

"She did. She's putting her feet up though. Exhausting day. Alright well, I just thought I'd check in. We'll speak again later."

"We will. Bye Dad." She looked up at Oliver.

"He says talking to Sikelela had got him over his own fake-passport. People do what they have to do, is his view now."

"They do, they do."

He drew her close.

Back at her telescope the next morning she began to feel as if something was going to explode. Something was going on she couldn't contain. She had landed in a nightmare from which there was no escape. She rang Sandra.

"Sandra, how are you, how is everyone? ....Might I drop in on you at the Centre this evening, or could we meet for coffee?...............Fine, five-thirty at the Centre. Look forward to seeing you."

Chapter Nineteen

As she entered through the glass door of the Reiki Centre and met the coolness and fragrance of whichever incense stick Sandra was burning, she felt herself enveloped by a sense of peace. Sandra called out to her to come through to the pantry. Her kettle was on and a Square Pants mug had coffee in it. She went through to meet a smiling Sandra, and flopped down in the chair she offered.

"You look a bit stressed," remarked Sandra. "Anything up?"

"Difficult to say. We, that is Dad and Mum and Oliver and I, met some children earlier this week, long story how, and have selected tentatively three or even four possible recipients. They don't know of course yet. We have realised now how flexible we are going to have to be, and that we are going to have to play it along by ear a lot of the time. We have no way of knowing how things will pan out with them, or whether we may have to pull out, or branch out! Peoples' actual stories are very complex. In any case no money is to be handed out directly. It will pay for costs."

"Yes, I can imagine. But why are you looking, well I would almost say frightened?"

"Sandra, I am utterly out of my depth. I'm twenty-six. I know nothing. Those kids were carrying the sorts of burdens I have no experience of at all. I was always looked after, and my way cleared. I never had to fight for things myself, and at times here we are winging it even where the law is concerned. At some stage I have to approach them again to discuss ways and means! How on earth do I set about it? We are working outside the system. There are no avenues of approach, or ways of dealing with these children you can learn from experts. It's just me making phone-calls, going up to London, meeting somewhere secretly without the parents knowing, and presenting plans which I don't know will work, and then somehow in any case, before we do anything, we have to talk to the parents. They will object. Their children, their lives. I am an intruder trying to tell them what to do, and offering to pay for it for God's sake! This is crazy Sandra. I wish John had just left me alone. I enjoyed our little conversations about a holistic approach to the body, and balance, and the higher levels of the Spirit. They left me feeling uplifted. I believed I was here for a purpose, but not a messy, possibly even illegal, purpose. I just had to be spiritual. You know, lift the vibrations, raise the dimension of the universe, be a light-bearer, a light-transmitter, feasible things like that. Not poking around in peoples domestic arrangements and telling them how to do things better. How impertinent is that!"

"Would you prefer a brandy?" asked Sandra

"Yeah..no. And I can't just hand in the towel. I've got Oliver wrestling with his conscience about the whole function of the law, and Dad, wise, and committed. He's not wrestling with anything, and Mum hoping we can pull this off decently without breaking the law, dear, but quite prepared to hide illegals, if that's what it takes. That's the stuff Louise was made of, Sandra. Never gave her nerves or her conscience a thought when it came to doing what had to be done. And I'm completely unable to carry this thing through, and the bloody money is in my account."

There was a long ominous pause, and then Sandra broke down in uncontrollable hysterics. She held on to the counter laughing till tears were running down her cheeks.

"Bridget, that was the most coherent letting-it-all-out I have ever heard! You were superb! I needed a recording of it for students to hear what living in the Spirit is really like. It's not about how to wash your crystals, you have to get dirty."

"Well I can't do a second take."

Sandra was off again.

"OK. let's look at it. Look at Christ first. He lived in the Spirit as you and I will never do in this life. Where did it get him? He was crucified. Take Mahatma Gandhi? He was shot. How do you think we are going to raise vibrations if we just sit on the edge of the pool in a lotus position without even getting wet? And we know something of what a muddy puddle the world is. There's the internet now. We all get a taste of it at times. But everything is One. We are part of, and of the stuff of, what we want to raise. We are It. In your life right now you have been sharing in imagination the lives of very young people who are struggling to raise themselves up. Raise themselves! If teenage kids can live in the stinking puddle, and with enormous courage, look up and see where it is they really want to go, but nothing is there to put their foot on to step up, and no hand is there to reach down and pull them up, how will they even start? You are the step up, or the hand reaching in to pull up. That's what you are Bridget. You don't have to be a miracle-worker. You just have to be there. What does the kid actually need? If you can provide that to a child on the brink of adult life you will change his whole life. You are looking at everything from a distance. Go close up. Go to London. You must have a contact number. Make contact. Meet in a crowded respectable cafe. Put your idea to the kid. If he or she oks it, ask to meet the parents. Put it to them. If they ok it, do it. If the kid refuses you can't use force. If the parents refuse, try another angle. I'm just sketching outlines here. Of course I don't know the details. It's one practical step after another. You are offering, not trying to force-feed, and the parents usually will know better than you do. If it's no, it's no. A teen-ager is a minor. You have no authority to act without the parents' consent. If they agree, get something in writing though. I would. Oliver could maybe draw up an agreement to be signed."

Bridget just gaped in silence for a minute.

"You're brilliant Sandra. Gosh. Aren't you ever frightened?"

"Of course! I am not even offering concrete financial assistance. I am offering spiritual energy Bridget. Think of the quagmire of misunderstanding that can get me into if I don't use the right words. This Centre smells beautiful, and the music is soothing, but as therapists we live on the edge. We depend on approval or 'likes' to keep the place even open! Anyway we love it. The day the public don't, we'll shut up shop."

"Thanks Sandra. You must be a whizz on the therapy table."

"Whatever I am, it's bad vibes to burst into hysterical laughter when your client pours out her agony. Sorry about that."

"No, you put it into perspective nicely. Sandra, going back to Michael, if we may. Has he got round his anxiety about the future of Ashcroft?"

"Yes, he was assured your father could not put in a claim now. His concern was theoretical for a possible future. He knows perfectly well your father isn't going to upsticks from Chedworth, and put in a claim for Ashcroft."

"No. I was thinking Sandra. John's letters, I can't destroy them. They are part of Ashcroft history really as well as ours. If I have children though I shan't share the Maria-John story with them. Grandfather never intended it to become common knowledge, instead of just rumour. So I'm thinking I will hand them over to you for whatever archives you have? There aren't many in fact. Only a few seem to have been preserved, and we have none of Maria's. Imagine Grandfather's pain on destroying them. I would like to have the records of his and Louise's experiences in South Africa for my children, but that's all. Maria's fragment of a journal belongs to Ashcroft, as does John's letter to her about the break-down. So, if I hand the bundle over to you, and you, would you, do printouts for me of the Africa letters, with any clue as to Maria's identity redacted, I would like to have them. We don't want to redact the affair. Just who it was. In that way we preserve the silence John maintained till the end. I shall suggest Dad gives you his real birth certificate to go in the archives."

Sandra looked at her consideringly.

"Alright, yes, I'll take them, and file them away. And I'll do printouts of the Africa letters with any clue as to Maria's identity redacted. That's it?"

"Yes, thankyou Sandra. I am sure that is the right thing to do. May I sound you out on another subject?"

"Of course." Sandra looked curious.

"John and Maria made a very close spiritual connection. Probably because they were separated physically they looked higher. And they seem to have found it Sandra. John speaks of them uniting in the light beaming down from the great central Sun. This was a spiritual Sun, not one you could pick out with a telescope. They united as one in the light, and channelled the spiritual light, apparently, down to earth. Does that sound a familiar thing to do?"

"Er yes. I wonder who trained John. It's a big subject. One aspect of it is that our universe is being flooded now with feminine energy. Another is that we are ascending from the third dimension to the fifth dimension. Another is that many of us are star-seeds, that is souls from other much more advanced planetary civilisations visiting this planet to raise its vibrational level, and rescue it from the mire of its' three dimensional darkness. Star-seeds incarnate here, so they don't remember where they came from. They just feel that Earth is not their home. They are supposed to awaken to their destiny, which is to be centres of light and channellers of light to our planet, and all who live on it. Another aspect is that, some say, there are spiritual forces of darkness battling against the beings of light, but they are already doomed. Our planet has arrived. Check out on you-tube. There are so many videos bearing messages to light-workers. The human family is awakening as from a dream, and light workers are developing a whole new energy. They see everything from the fifth dimension point of view, and have brought their energy here from their home planet. Others, not star-seeds, accept the new higher dimensional energy entering our planet, and thereby also rise to the fifth dimension. Check out star-seeds, light-workers, and ascension on you tube. It's just like googling the symptoms of altzheimers. You will definitely start to fantasise you are a star seed."

Bridget stared into the distance.

"Well, I did ask. Do you consider yourself to be a light-worker?"

"Yes, but I avoid the lime-light. The moment there is a suggestion of higher spiritual levels, crowds of followers barge in claiming that they too are of this advanced elite. They too are ascended beings. They consider themselves to be special very sensitive people who are too spiritually advanced for others to understand. This ascension process is giving them headaches, and sweats, and all sorts of side-effects, which are not understood by those not tuned up to their vibrational level. From time to time they will rest in bed with the blinds down to recover from the discomfort caused by the energy."

"Gosh. Do they have that written in their sick notes?"

"The actual ascension process *is* going on, but the New Age hoo-ha has created a fake spiritual elite. They believe they are far more advanced than the masses embroiled in their blind three-D occupations. 'They are not as I am'".

"The Pharisee with his nose in the air."

"Precisely. Jesus called those of his time hypocrites. They were devoid of true compassion. We can all look down kindly on someone we believe to be inferior, but Jesus washed the disciples' feet as a demonstration that there is no such thing as an elite, not even in this three-D world. I may be Lady Sandra, but what does that mean? Nothing much. It is a label denoting something in the history of my husband's family. Even he, bless him, usually forgets he is Sir Michael. (Whatever unease he may have had about your father, it's not about being called Sir). I do not believe myself to be a star-seed but I could be. So could you. I have received no authoritative intimation as to my other-planetary lineage so I just get on with my daily humdrum life. Being Jeremy and Natasha's Mum matters infinitely more to me than wondering whether I came from Sirius. I do practise light channelling in meditation though. That is very far from being hogwash. I believe very much that it is crucial work for those who know it exists, and have a flair for it. But I would never mention it in public, because of the sickening, nauseating, drivel people come out with. I distance myself completely from pretence, and say nothing."

"So you wouldn't welcome me as a disciple or a sycophant." Bridget grinned.

"Why? Do you want to be one?"

"No, but would you recommend a book on that sort of meditation please? I would like to have a go."

"Of course. I'll give you one. Shall you rope Oliver in?"

"Not right now. He is still grappling with aberrations in the law."

"And in any case he has you down here. He doesn't have to look for you up there."

"Exactly, and in any case, also, he is a lawyer. It's his job. Wouldn't you rather see him sort out a few injustices in the legal system, than channel light down on us from the great central Sun? I would!"

"I certainly would."

"Though, bearing in mind, John was in the thick of it, big time, in the messiness of the three-D world, while at the same time channelling down light from the central Sun."

"Yes, that's what made him something of a Saint I think. A Saint was one who blended the material and the mystical so effectively that he or she could alter the substance of the material. "

"You mean like trans-substantiation?"

"No. There it is the faith of the believer which enables him to receive the bread and the wine as a sacrament. Without faith it doesn't deliver. It doesn't transmute, in my view."

"You see John as having been maybe a Saint?"

"Well, in inverted commas, yes, He didn't qualify for a halo, but his presence must have been sacramental."

"And Maria?"

"The same I think."

"I'm having a wonderful time Sandra. Thankyou. I have never had anyone in my life before I could talk about these things with, except of course my grandfather himself. Maybe it was he who set me off on my spiritual journey? My guru?"

"It does seem like it. "

"Who set you off on yours?"

"My mother of course. She took the things of the spirit as manifestly obvious. She talked to angels. You'ld think she was talking to you, and then realise there was an angel present, 'he's standing by the fire-place Sandra.'"

"Well I have taken up far too much of your time. Jeremy and Natasha will be wondering where you've got to. Thankyou for everything Sandra. I can see why Maria talked to you."

Chapter Twenty

Bridget left the Reiki Centre feeling as if she was floating. She felt light-headed. She went straight to her car and drove home. She had barely got through the door when her phone rang. It was Zola. She wanted to report that she had told her parents she was taking piano lessons from a friend. They didn't need persuading to meet the family. They were most anxious to. As it turned out they knew Joseph's mother from meeting her in church, and they formed an immediate bond. Zola's parents told them that if they allowed her to take piano lessons Zola had promised to work very hard in future to get good grades at school. A lady she had met at a school function had said she could get her a piano if her parents were willing, so they planned to accept that. They would however employ a teacher to come to their house. Bridget exclaimed with pleasure and asked her to text her her address. She would let her know when to expect the piano. She would also write to her parents to explain how it was she was she was giving away a piano. After that she would wait to see how the lessons went, and possibly arrange for another teacher later.

Thank goodness Oliver was coming. She needed to unwind, or rewind, she wasn't sure which, but she felt hyper-stimulated.

He arrived wearing corduroys and light-weight green sweater. She held him tightly for a while drawing on his strength, so reassuring when you were all of a do-da, which she was, somehow. He was very curious to know why she was distrait, and even a little fey when she lifted the kettle over the coffee jar to pour.

"No, no, I'm fine. Zola has told her parents about the piano lessons, and has got permission to have proper lesson at home on the piano I shall send. So that is step one with her. We'll just wait now to see if she blossoms."

"That's wonderful. So what else?"

"Let's just sit quietly minute with our coffees while I collect my thoughts. It's alright. I've been talking to Sandra. Just need to recoup. Everything's fine."

Oliver looked at her keenly, as he put down his mug on the coaster. Something had changed. She had gained some sort of inner poise but seemed flustered on the outside. What had Sandra been telling her?"

Finally she put her coffee down and told him,

"I seem to have had something of an epiphany. It's hard to describe. I went to see Sandra, partly to ask her to put Grandfather's letters in the

Featherstone archives. The Kendall archives isn't the place for them because we don't have history as such. Maria does. Plus he never intended our family to read them! They are about Maria. I also felt that if there is any anxiety about an illegitimate son in the Featherstone house they will be comfortable if all the evidence is with them. I shall suggest Dad gives me his real birth certificate to go there. It happened. It was amazing, but it was private. Sandra will do print-outs for me of the Africa bits with anything pointing to Maria's identity redacted."

"Well that seems to be a solution. I wondered where you would put them. Go on."

"So then, you know I wanted to ask her what the spiritual union thing might be, well I did. An avalanche fell on me. Looking back I think the whole subject is so vast she didn't know where to start, so she just fired off the whole thing in about a dozen rounds, yaker yaker yaker yaker. I sat there shell-shocked. I should have taken notes, except in any case she went too fast. The first thing, as I remember is that there is a whole new flood of super fifth dimensional energy invading and taking over our planet, and also an inrush of feminine energy (to balance the masculine one which is already in situ, as we know). This energy comes from, I think, far higher spiritual dimensions than the one we currently inhabit, which is known as the three D, the shelf-life of which has expired."

Oliver was starting to laugh.

"I had Sandra in hysterics earlier, over my identity crisis. Let me focus. There are numerous and vast planetary civilisations going back aeons before the birth of our planet, and those civilisations are infinitely more advanced than ours. Souls from higher dimensions have been incarnating on Earth to assist our ascension up, namely to the fifth." She looked at him as a school teacher looks at her class to check they are abreast.

Oliver was nearly falling off his chair.

"It's really gratifying to have one's audience falling off their seats. This is my second time today. So here we are, breathing in this light, and fifth dimensional energy, without most of us noticing anything unusual. I was breathless as I left her salon I have to admit. My head was spinning, but I put it down to shock. There is a hitch. Super dark forces are out there trying to destroy the forces of light, but they are already doomed because occupation by the light is a fait accompli. "

"Right," said Oliver. "So we don't have to worry on that score."

"No. But as individuals we have the choice to align ourselves with the dark or the light. The planet may be going up, but I can sit sulking and refuse to budge. That is an option. However, these superior beings know we are not an easy pitch, hence their decision to incarnate here to sell it to us. These souls are called star-seeds, because, Oliver? they come from the stars. They teach that Earth's vibrational speed is increasing at the speed, literally, of light, and we don't want to miss our space flights. There are however, and Sandra is seriously stressed out about this, those who having sensed there is a new elite on the block, have hastened to sign up, and are now fanning themselves, complaining about the energy. They lie down apparently sometimes in darkened rooms to survive the impact. Seriously. She wants to tell them to get a life. In her view they are the modern equivalent to the Pharisees Jesus called hypocrites who complimented themselves that others were 'not as I am'. Thus, these people, in exactly the same way, believe they are from highly advanced civilisations slumming it here, and having to suffer the hoi polloi who have no clue about the ascension and about the side-effects endured by those who are in the know that we are going up. And incidentally, apparently, forgotten that if so, they were meant to be serving. Sandra pointed out that Jesus taught there is no spiritual elite. That was what his washing of the disciples' feet was about."

"Bridget! What utter tosh!" exclaimed Oliver.

"Yes, you would think, but Sandra is firm that the narrative itself is absolutely kosher. It's just the fakes who are making a pigs' dinner of it. She says she is a light worker herself, but never breathes a word for fear of alerting any acolytes. I didn't get round to asking if she is part of any society or whether she does it alone. I respect her sense of vocation one hundred per cent Oliver. She is doing what she claims she is doing, just as John and Maria were. We wouldn't know a thing about theirs if we hadn't read his letters. And we know Maria and she talked."

"So what has flustered you?" asked Oliver. "Are you experiencing a touch of space sickness?"

"Oliver, she is so down to earth. I went there ready to explode with worry about this funding work. How can I cope? Who am I to....? I'm not cut out for this. I was in a spin, and she punctured that hot air in seconds. I was restored to my own equilibrium. Just take it a day at a time. Then she pumped me with all this fifth dimensional ether, and I started to float. Literally I had a sensation of floating. And that is what has flustered me. She is going to lend me a book on meditation, but on the grass-roots level there are ramifications to ascension, just as Jesus' disciples realised, it costs. Selfishness, greed, vanity, they are all characteristics of three D living. They are done now. Those attitudes are no longer viable. That world has gone. Now it is one for all and all for one. We are one. That was what Iyana was talking about essentially. She visualises forming groups of ten or twelve people she called brigades or fellowships, which would band together, and whenever anyone was in trouble the others would be honour-bound to come to their aid. That was, essentially also, like Louise's group. Iyana used the words, 'all for one and one for all'. That is fifth dimensional living. I shall practise some meditation along the lines of, I hope, John's, whatever that was. And I need to discover what 'one for all' means in my life. I hope you won't dump me for talking such tosh Oliver," she said anxiously.

He came and sat beside her, and put his arm round her.

"Darling, what do you think I am wrestling with if not to discover how the law can serve as well as punish, without losing the control a good punishment delivers to the seriously criminal? Society has to be protected, and the punishment must fit the crime, but should petty things like birth certificates," he crossed himself, "ruin someone's life? John said no. Richard and your Mum said no, and I say no. But there it is. It is a certificate, sanctified by the law. These are just fragments of things I am looking at."

"John said they would fudge their way through with the fake. Of course he meant Louise would fudge, with her street smarts. So you are alright with me living for all?"

"Well, yeah, as long as you put me first, naturally. The hoi polloi can have what they like after I have had my share."

"Oh good, because I am thinking of lending Coleridge Grange to the police as a women's shelter, to include children too of course. After all, we have three houses, and he who hath only two coats is expected to give one to someone who has none."

"Now *I* am feeling breathless," complained Oliver. "Are there any more after-shocks to follow, or is that pretty much it for now?"

"That's all I can remember off the top of my head."

"It's a great idea, Bridget, but have you considered whether Lydney would appreciate women from violent, say, homes, attracting, possibly, the criminal element, to contaminate their unspoiled idyll?"

"But the whole point is that it would be secret, Oliver. It would be a sanctuary. A safe house. Anyway, can Lydney claim to be crime free?"

"I don't know, but I say go for it. If it is shouted down you can think again."

"I can."

"But nothing noisy. Leafy neighbourhoods won't stomach that."

"Are you laughing at me?"

"No. Just looking at it from all angles."

"What do you really think about the New Age spirituality and me training to meditate?"

"I am open to the notion that as a planet we are being raised to a higher vibrational level, because of Dion Fortune, of whom I am a fan. I have browsed around and read about Edgar Cayce and Mrs. Blavatsky. Sandra says her mother is a psychic and I believe her of course. And currently we have the case of John and Maria which I believe implicitly. Sandra herself. So, fine, of course study meditation, but I think you are half-way there already out on your back lawn every morning." Bridget smiled.

"Anything yet on Sikelela? Or is Dad going to take the lead on handling that?"

"I rang him earlier. I think we shall deal with it jointly. He plans to go up to London to the boy's home, and talk to his uncle and aunt. He is the one with the rapport with them. I am his back-up to sort out the legalities."

"And possibly the one to find some decent professional document-forgerers."

"Now you are laughing at me. What I am looking for is a legal way of getting him British nationality. Uuka and Akhona are down as his parents. Do I treat that as the truth, and go from there? I can't betray them. That, for what it is worth, is fixed. So I will try getting him a British passport. See if objections are raised. Richard is going to find out about their residential status. They are here legally, so must have visas, and can probably get British passports, along with their children, if they don't already have them. I'm waiting for the results of Richard's visit. We will fix it somehow Bridget. Sikelela will get his chance, and we will help out his uncle and aunt with the costs of his higher education."

"That is so good. And we are left with the lovely Iyana. I will look into that. The ultimate objective is to get a home-help-cum-nanny into her home, so she can study for university. Shall we move on and have supper now? It's fish and chips I bought on the way home." Oliver rubbed his hands appreciatively.

"Nothing like fish and chips to restore the morale!"

Later, after washing their plates they returned to the parlour. Bridget drew the curtains and put on a light. Her mobile rang. It was Sandra.

"Hi Bridget, are you recuperating from your catharsis?"

"I might have been, thanks, Sandra if the after-care had been more soothing, like, you know, you're fine, everything's fine, relax, instead of giving me the news of alien invasions by different races, some good, some bad, and hinting that, possibly, we don't know for sure, but, maybe, I might not be entirely human myself? Will my ship come to take me back home to Sirius one day is my new worry, if that is my planet? However, a large plate of fish and chips has restored the balance, thanks. So I'm good. Oh, and Oliver is here talking about the iniquities of the legal system, so that scared away the bogey-men. How are you?"

Sandra was laughing again.

"You are a caution, as my Mum would say. I was ringing to ask if you and Oliver can come to dinner tomorrow night?"

"We'd love to come Sandra, Thanks.......Oliver says thank you."

"Lovely. Will seven suit you? See you then."

Chapter Twenty-One

Oliver stayed the night, and kept to his bed until Bridget had gone in for her shower. Then he too went down to make a coffee and go outside to stand on the lawn. He watched the clouds a bit. It was easy to float along with them in spirit and view the things of this world from their point of view. Which did not, and could not, diminish the vital importance of the lives of the human beings living in it. He would, he hoped, fight to the death for the rights of the smallest of these people as Jesus had done. The least of these was greatest in the kingdom of heaven whatever dimensional level the kingdom of heaven resided in. He would live alongside one of the least of these, rather than inhabit some posh residence in the fifth dimension. He knew he sounded daft, even to himself, but he meant it. That was the road John had taken. The most vulnerable of the black community was worth giving his life for, and he had indeed offered up, potentially, his life, and at the very least his reputation. He questioned the spirituality of anyone who claimed a seat at the high table when the better place was with the hoi polloi at the bottom end of the lowest table. That was what Bridget and Sandra had been saying, and he subscribed to it. Eventually, after having set his compass, he returned to the kitchen.

Bridget was downstairs, and in her day clothes. She put on some toast.

"Will you have an egg, or two, Oliver?" she asked.

"Yes, I'll prepare them. How shall you have yours?"

"Fried please."

"Your house or mine this evening?"

"Yours? We can do them alternately, but let's unwind at Jesse's first. Oh no! I forgot, we're going to Sandra's to dinner."

"We can meet at Jesse's at five-fifteen. Then each go to our own houses to get ready, and I will pick you up here at ten to seven. Will that work?"

They each had keys to both houses, and Bridget left first to go to the Institute. She took in a deep breath as she started the car. Good to get back to the things of the earth! Maria too might have been into some sort of transcendental meditation but her heart was in her botanical garden. Hers too would always be with Nature.

The day passed by quite quickly for her. She loved the companionship of her colleagues. They shared her world of the mind and they understood each other. With Marjorie, a woman in her forties, she had developed a friendship and they would sometimes go on for coffee together after work, at least until she met Oliver. She realised guiltily that she had been neglecting her friend recently. During the lunch-break she sat with her and acknowledged that she had been preoccupied lately.

"Well you were off for a fortnight so there hasn't been much opportunity for a gossip," said Marjorie. "How are things going? I gathered your grandfather had died and there were things to settle?"

"Yes, that's right. It has been very complicated. He left me some money to use to support three under-privileged South African children's education. He lived most of his life in Cape Town. So working out the logistics of how that might be done has been the main job, really."

"It must be. How on earth do you set about that? And here was me, thinking romantically, that you had found a glamorous new boy-friend."

"Oh well, that too. I have. He's the solicitor involved in Grandfather's affairs."

"Well glad to hear it! Mostly I have to rush off home to pick up the children from child-care and I'm worrying I don't have much time to be a proper friend to other women these days. Children take over your life. They become your life in the end, but I love my gossips with you. I feel young again, with time to be frivolous!" Bridget laughed.

"Well there are no children on my horizon yet, but we are semi-living together. Two houses of course."

"I'm so pleased Bridget! That's great. And we will meet when we can."

Oliver's car drew up at six-fifty and she went out to join him. She wasn't worried about what she was wearing this time. Sandra knew her too well to be looking her up and down. She had put on a straight flower-designed dress with her gold chain.

Michael came to the door to greet them, and the children were behind him. They seemed pleased to see her, thought Bridget happily. Sandra called a welcome from the drawing-room door.

"We have kept your grandfather's photo on display," she said quietly. "We seem to have got to know him so much better recently, and he is after all, as it were, one of the family."

"Is that what you tell Jeremy and Natasha?"

"No. To them he is a very old friend of the family and your grandfather. They aren't bothered anyway."

Michael was much more forthcoming than he had been on her previous visits, but Bridget realised he appreciated the presence of Oliver to balance his group. He and Oliver got on well.

They shared anecdotes about local families and properties, and Bridget was content to listen and laugh or exclaim. It was all so homely.

She relaxed and talked to the children, realising for the first time that they were cousins. Did they share any physical likeness? she wondered.

They went in for dinner at eight, and although it was set formally, what they actually ate was fairly simple, grilled salmon, roast chicken, roast potatoes, broccoli roasted with olive oil, garlic, and lemon, a cucumber creamy salad, followed by trifle. Whew! Oliver and Bridget both complimented Sandra on the sumptuous meal.

"Glad you liked it," she said. "healthy food is Nature's cure for most things."

"Is that what your Mum said," asked Bridget, grinning.

"She did indeed! Now children I need you to go upstairs and attend to your home-work. We have things to talk about."

Bridget glanced at Oliver in alarm. He just smiled a little, as if to say it's alright.

The four of them returned to the sitting-room where a long-shaped wrapped parcel had been placed on the coffee-table.

"Bridget," said Sandra, "between the four of us we don't have to pretend any more. You are Maria's darling grand-daughter. She tried to hide it from you, but she loved you. She left you her house. The problem was she could not know how things would develop. Richard himself had of course heard the rumours, but ignored them as gossip. We have here an heirloom Maria wanted you to have, but when she was alive she had no means of giving it to you, so she confided in Michael. Michael wasn't stunned either. She asked him to give it to you, if ever the right moment came, when you knew your ancestry and would be friendly enough towards her to like to accept it. That time has come. Michael thought it wisest to leave it in Francis's care, so he did. He didn't tell me as it was Maria's business. When you came here to show him the ring and the chess-piece he knew you were on the road to discovery, and presumably on the prompting of John. They were the clues he sent you. You rang his colleague in Cape Town, and he recovered the letter to be sent if you asked. And you and I found the bundles of letters and papers in the attic. The story all came tumbling out. You claimed the house she had given you. Michael had in fact checked up on it from time to time with Timothy, and paid the Council Tax this year. I believe Timothy told you. Otherwise he acted on your grandmother's instructions. He is not in the family loop."

Sandra picked up the parcel, and gave it to Bridget.

"And she wanted you to have this. Your great-grandmother wore it I believe on the occasion of Queen Victoria's wedding? It was much loved by the ladies in your family, and they passed it down to their daughters. So, here, on behalf of Maria, I pass it down to you. Open it,"

Bridget glanced at Oliver who smiled back encouragingly.

"Did you know?" she asked,

"No, not at all. I just saw Michael calling on Francis, which wasn't surprising since Francis is his solicitor."

She had the paper off now, and inside there was a long brown old jewellery box. She opened it and nestled in faded white satin was a chain and pendant. She gasped. It was fabulous! It was a fine gold chain in three articulated sections connected with cut diamonds, and pearls. The pendant was equally finely crafted, and set with tiny diamonds, and a little pearl was suspended beneath. It was stunning. She had seen things like this only in museums."

Sandra had not seen it before, and she exclaimed too.

"That is so amazing Bridget and not even dated. People wear cheap versions of this sort of thing all the time."

"I don't think I shall dare wear it," said Bridget. "This is very costly indeed."

"Well you must wear it now," said Sandra firmly, "let me put it on for you." She took the chain from Bridget's hand and clasped it round her neck." Bridget smiled, embarrassed, and incline to cry, but checking herself.

"Come and see in the mirror," said Sandra, so she got up and looked in the mirror over the fire-place, For a moment, she thought, had she looked like Maria? Or was it Maria for a moment looking at her through her own eyes and smiling?"

"Was that Maria?" she muttered to Sandra.

"For a second? Yes I think so," said Sandra.

"Does anybody else know Maria left this for me?"

"No. There is nobody *to* know. Wear it. If anybody asks, say it is a family heirloom and your grandmother gave it to you."

"Yes of course. Do I need to put it in a bank?"

"Give it to your solicitor to put somewhere, like Maria did," grinned Sandra.

"I will do that."

"How well did you know Maria, Michael?" asked Bridget.

He shifted in his chair a little.

"Well she was my Aunt, so on that family level I knew her very well. I was not good at gardens, as I still am not, but she used to take me round a bit talking about the plants. She made very good fruit drinks, and used to serve them in the garden on summery days."

"Oh yes! She did. I remember that too. There was a delicious one made from strawberries."

"And another from raspberries!" said Michael, "when they were in season. Everything had to be fresh-picked."

"It was like that in our house too. We lived in Rose Cottage, you remember. I used to see you all."

"We played croquet on the lawn, in the time-honoured fashion. Uncle Roger was very good at it. I have no recollection of John of course, but his imprint was very much here."

"How so?" asked Bridget curiously. "He never mentioned Ashcroft himself if he could avoid it. We found letters of his. Sandra will have filed them away here somewhere. From them we know Ashcroft and Roger and Maria were constantly in his thoughts, till the end."

"He was so much part of what went on here in his young days at Brook's. He was instrumental in much of the major re-building and re-shaping of the estate when we had to re-invent ourselves as a thriving business if we were to survive. He had the shrewd practical head Roger lacked. Without John I'm not sure Ashcroft would have survived. He knew what would work and what wouldn't, and Roger had implicit faith in his judgement. After he left, Roger always gave John credit for the development of the gardens and the Centre. Roger was charming and attracted people to this place, but he didn't have the common touch. Not that the Featherstones are an ancient family, but he had led a very sheltered life. Maria's family was much older, in the recorded sense. We all go back to the Stone Age and developed together, but somehow she liked Roger. Well, we know how much she liked him now. She cared for him through thick and thin."

"Michael," said Bridget awkwardly, "did he really never suspect anything, do you think? Did they really hood-wink him? He may not have had a good business head but he wasn't daft. He was shrewd in his own way."

"Thankyou for saying that, Bridget. Yes he was. He shouldn't be under-estimated in our memories. He was incapacitated after his breakdown, and by the time he was getting his life back John had gone. Don't you think, probably, that he might have felt deeply ashamed at having embarrassed John so badly? He knew John well enough to know he would have been dismayed to be so misunderstood. In fact the letter John wrote to him later was beautiful. I think he didn't know. He had been fantasising too much when he was here, so never had the chance to reassess what had really happened, and his wife of course nurtured him back to wholeness, bless her, really. In those days he could have been a laughing-stock (the staff here all knew) but she gave him face. She out-stared, so to speak, anybody who might show disrespect. Not that on the whole anyone did. He was well-liked. "

144

"Yes," said Bridget, "probably you are right. I really hope so."

"So do I Bridget, John and Maria both gave their lives to protecting him."

"Well, I think, no regrets Michael. Look at John's life in South Africa! We don't know whether they would have lived happily ever after. Soul mates don't always, I believe. Too much of a good thing or something. They kept their love, and they lived their lives to the full. I believe all is well, and all is very well, as Mother Julian would say."

"Amen to that," said Sandra.

"Thank you, John and Maria, for showing me what it takes to live authentically," said Oliver.

"Thank you, from me too, for bringing me such a wonderful new friend," said Sandra.

"Thank you, Roger and Maria, for your legacy. I pray I will live up to it and do it proud," said Michael

"Thank you, Grandmother and Grandfather, for all that you have passed on to your family, and taught each of us what are the important things in life," said Bridget.

The four of them saluted the ancestors with pretend glasses.

About the Author

Jennifer Hashmi was born in Bradford in 1938 and educated at Bingley Grammar School. She trained as a speech therapist, and later took a theology course. From1964 she served as a Parish Worker in the Church of North India. In 1977 she married Salman Hashmi who was principal of a Delhi University College. They had two children. After his passing she returned to Britain in 2005. She has four grand-children.

Ingram Content Group UK Ltd.
Milton Keynes UK
UKHW020045210623
423745UK00014B/416